BLOOD

BLOOD

Stories at the Dark Edges of Love

NIGEL PEACE

ISBN 978-1-910027-45-5

Typesetting by Wordzworth Ltd
www.wordzworth.com

Cover design by Titanium Design Ltd
www.titaniumdesign.co.uk

Cover image:
Human Heart, Adobe Images

Published by Local Legend
www.local-legend.co.uk

**LOCAL
LEGEND**

For you.

May you find the love that never changes.

About the Author

Nigel Peace has walked a full life, with a foot in each of two worlds – the earthly and the paranormal – which can be pretty uncomfortable. Engineer and social worker, tour guide in Cold War Russia and mathematics teacher, he has also devoted years of study in depth to the improbable and the downright impossible (as most people see things).

Along the way he has been blessed to know love in many forms. Well, perhaps not always blessed, although they do say we grow with every kind of relationship… perhaps… if we choose to.

Nigel's website is www.spiritrevelations.com

This Book

This collection of stories, with a few poems, has emerged through a lifetime's experience of finding, losing, observing and imagining love in its many forms. But don't expect any cosy romance here. Because love rarely shapes up as we hope or believe it will. This writing is at the dark edges of those shapes.

And if you read it in bed at night, you are sure to have some very strange and revealing dreams...

Previous Publications

Fiction

Signs of Life   ISBN 978-1-907203-20-6
An afterlife comedy, as our deceased heroes race to sabotage the angels' very bad Grand Plan for humanity.

Broken Sea   ISBN 978-1-910027-23-3
A heart-wrenching love story set in the dangerous days of the Warsaw Pact invasion of Czechoslovakia.

Non–Fiction

Spirit Revelations   ISBN 978-1-907203-14-5
Hundreds of accounts of true prophetic dreams and everyday synchronicities, proving that we can know the future and receive spiritual guidance.

Lighting the Path   ISBN 978-1-907203-26-8
A down-to-earth companion to the I Ching, showing with many examples how to use and understand the greatest oracle known to Man.

These titles are published by Local Legend.
www.local-legend.co.uk

Contents

Images

An Accidental Pelican

Each morning she would push the last corner of her croissant around the plate with one finger, as though trying to decide the best position for it. This would go on for two or three minutes. She had the air of a woman who needed things to be in their place. Always neatly dressed, her clothes were light, of course, in white and pastels, yet discrete, classy. The right leg would be crossed over the left, away from him, with her sandal pointing down. Classic body language. Her long fair hair was touched by the sun but always soft and combed, tied with a white ribbon. A woman who took care over how the world might see her.

And then she would appear to lose patience and flick the scraps of pastry onto the ground for the chi chi, the grassquits. If you hadn't seen the same familiar pattern being played out every morning, you'd think there were deeply troubling thoughts in her mind. Naturally, he would now smile and shift in his seat as though this were a signal, drain his espresso and gesture towards me for more. It had been like this long before this one arrived although, had he been asked, he would have been quite sure that he'd made the decision himself.

Still, the final bill was already written up. After a while, if you watch something long enough, you get to know how it's likely to turn out.

"How did it turn out last night? Did you enjoy yourself?"

"Jerk."

"I'm sorry?"

"Like all the others."

The morning before, she had had told him about the American. You might wonder why she would do that, yet it was all part of her life's silky web. The story went that she'd been leaving the sports centre and just happened to pause at Reception to check her bookings for the week, when she had seen him… No, she had "felt him" behind her with some strange, otherworldly sense and had been paralysed by this gentle energy surrounding her as he watched from the other side of the foyer. I know. Even I winced at this one but I suppose it made for good conversation. So, he'd approached slowly and come to stand beside her just outside the doors as she searched her bag for the car keys. That part was quite clever. His brown eyes were deep and Latin, he had a soft smile that hesitated as though he were too shy to let the words out, he wore a designer suit that was a little loose on his slim… you know the sort of thing. And within minutes they had arranged dinner.

At least, that's what she thought. At least, that's what she said she thought. But it turned out that she was the menu and – he had politely apologised – his yacht had to leave on the morning tide. Unavoidable business. Surely it should have been obvious? Men like that don't live on this island. The ones who live here are mostly those who scratch a sort of living from the rocky land, who spend a couple of months each year clearing up after the storms and rebuilding their timber and corrugated iron homes, and the people like me and her who make a sort of living from him and the others who arrive and leave on yachts.

"I'm sorry."

"It's not your fault. Except that you're a man."

He'd lapsed into an uncomfortable silence, probably struggling with the idea of carrying the can for his entire gender when all he was trying to do was be her friend. That last bit was almost certainly what he told himself.

"But I'm your friend, too," he said. And at this point – the use of that word was the trigger – it was inevitable that she would lift her head slightly from the sand with its tufts of rough grass and hidden, sleeping clouds of chitras, and raise her eyes demurely towards him in that way no straight man can resist. If only we hadn't evolved so successfully and developed such clever manners to facilitate our social interactions, we might not have lost the ability to see what lies beneath the surface.

By the way, only the female sandfly bites.

"Yes, I know," she'd smiled at last. "In fact, I think you're the only man who's ever actually listened to me." Grief, I had to turn away so that my raised eyebrows wouldn't be noticed and busy myself with drying glasses and rearranging bowls of pistachios.

Mind you, credit where it's due, he was doing pretty well, this one. By now it had been about ten days since he'd arrived, a bit pasty and carrying a few pounds but quiet and courteous for a tourist. A bit of an enigma, perhaps. It was always rare for a visitor to be alone, for one thing. Usually, it was loud groups of Americans or small groups of yacht man. You'd get the occasional loved-up couple who'd saved up for their special holiday, all smiles and hand-holding until they realised they hadn't done their research properly. People like that normally go to one of the bigger islands where the facilities are more developed and the local poverty less in their faces.

So this one was interesting, maybe with a particular reason for coming here that he wasn't telling me when I'd asked politely. You'd see him early in the morning, swimming for twenty minutes from the hotel beach then sitting on a rock with a cigarette to watch the circling frigates and the occasional diving pelican as though mesmerised, before going to get dressed and walking along here for breakfast. She would arrive mid-morning after the early lessons and sit alone nearby, as she always had. As usual, it only took a couple of days for her to look across, and that was enough for him to offer her another coffee. But he was different, yes, the Englishman. He did listen. And he hadn't made a move.

"Where are you from?" he'd asked that first day. They always ask that. "You speak beautifully." They always say that too, but it was true. Though she never quite answered the question – it was always some vague throwaway reference to Europe – her voice was clear and correct, the accent intriguing and enticing at the same time, the words educated and practised. She was cultured, anyone could see that, and she was probably far more intelligent than nearly anyone she would meet here. Yes, of course, there are different kinds of intelligence. And presumably she had a past too, which may be why she never quite answered that sort of question. Whatever it was, it lay well hidden beneath the surface.

"Have you lived here long?" he'd asked the second day. It took a day to get to the next question they always ask because, at first, the time spent sharing espressos was mostly silent. She controlled this space, almost as though tolerating his presence, that supposed strange inner sense of hers watching warily, trying to make him out. He was very different, quiet, courteous and undemanding. She wouldn't have been used to this, a man who didn't seem to want anything.

"Too long," she answered wryly, as always. But it was clear to those of us who lived here that she would never leave the island. It had been more than ten years anyway, arriving with the boyfriend who'd had a new job at the marina. That's as much as she told him at first. "But he turned out like all the others."

"Why, was he unfaithful?"

You could read any man's thoughts at this point. 'No, surely that wasn't possible. Who could not want her? Who could ever leave her?' So here was another trigger word and she shook her head slightly and got up to leave, for all the world declaring that the question was too painful. And as she walked slowly in that measured way to her car, he would have decided for himself that no, surely no man could leave her. She was tall and gently muscled, her clothes lightly brushing her tanned skin and making little effort to hide her figure. She was a goddess. Poena, perhaps, the attendant to Nemesis.

On the third day, with neither greeting nor preamble, and presumably having mulled him over and decided to take him further, she told the story.

"He was spending more and more time at work. Out with clients, that sort of thing, so he said. He didn't listen to me, didn't ask how my day went. Didn't want to understand what I needed from this place. Then one day he'd gone out and left his laptop open... Well, what was I supposed to do? He clearly wanted me to, didn't he? So I looked at the search history and found that he'd been on a dating site for months. Described himself as single, naturally. And with his boat trips around the islands he could easily..." A slight gesture of one hand invited us to imagine the rest.

"That's awful."

"Of course it is. I mean, fidelity is absolute, isn't it? He tried to say it was all just to pass the time, to have – can you believe – conversations with people because you don't get to meet many people on the island. People like us. As if I wasn't enough for him." It's true, the opportunities are limited on an island, though you probably know that before you come, don't you? And at this point any man would have thought, 'Well, you'd be enough for me.' This man resisted.

"What did you do?"

"So naturally I did the same thing, set up my own account and gave myself a new name, changed a few details, just to see how he'd like it."

"I'm guessing he didn't."

"He's still here. A sad loner who can't commit."

"You still see him, then?"

"From time to time. You can't help it here. But he doesn't mean anything anymore. It's just sex."

That wasn't what he'd meant by the question, nor was it the answer he'd expected. He had lapsed into the familiar silence again, probably wondering whether this had all been some kind of warning. Or invitation. My, how often had I watched from the shadows as this game played itself out...

Φ

There are no seasons on this island, a steady twenty-six to thirty degrees or so and more than three hundred days of sunshine. Then there's the threat of storms, perhaps the odd hurricane, in what people call autumn.

Apparently, though the idea is as foreign to local people as snow, it's some kind of tax haven. This accounts for the yachts and the cluster of modern stone buildings in the centre of town like alien thumbs among the handful of wooden shop fronts, many of them boarded up. Most of those fine buildings have bars on the ground floor windows and the tallest, most heavily muscled local man that could be found standing proudly at the door in a dark uniform with a bulge in his jacket. Some of them are shops selling French designs, with fake but attractive paintings beside the full-length mirrors on the walls.

A little way outside town there's the sports centre, with swimming pool, sauna, aerobics… everything the unfit wealthy might want. And a few hotels, from the exclusive and bijoux to the pretty basic yet as expensive as the owners dare. Tourists come because they want some warmth or to get away from something, or someone. It comes to the same thing. But it's always a pay-off, isn't it, between what you think you want and what your soul needs.

Unless we are extremely unfortunate, we are all born into a world of contrast, of moving seasons, of light and darkness, of joy and despair, of warmth and cold, of fertility and wilderness. These are the things that define life on our planet, with all the changes and uncertainties that teach us what it means to be truly human. The modestly successful are those who embrace all this and who suffer faithfully, if not gladly, in the knowledge that there will surely be another time, another change, another season. These are the ones who keep their hearts open and share this life with others, rejoicing in their happiness and comforting them in their sorrows, who retreat into quietness when times are frugal and live frugally when times are comfortable.

Then there are those who find the inevitable darkness all too painful and close their shutters, who neither express their pain (whilst believing themselves to be life's victims) nor are willing to share in others'. Many of them spend their time wondering how things would be if only some great stroke of good fortune came their way, since life appears to be entirely a matter of cosmic chance. You will find some of these hiding away in their homes or in like-minded groups, whilst some try to escape the cold by looking for a new home where their own selves cannot find them.

Two kinds of people. Well, sorry, no, there are three kinds. There are those born into what the second kind call a 'paradise', like this island. We could include, perhaps, its frozen opposite. These have a life without seasons, without the opportunity for growth, with narrow boundaries that almost never change. They generally become morose and unkind, unless they are intelligent or paradoxically – some would say perversely – blessed with humanity, in which case they bravely leave as soon as possible and make way for those others who pour excitedly into the spaces they have left and fill them up. And wonder why they did. And then what's to be done, and where is it all leading?

Φ

After a couple of days, and perhaps despite himself, he couldn't help venturing the inevitable next move, ignoring the warning signs.

"So do you live alone now?"

"I love my work. Always new people to see, coming off the boats. Some regulars too, of course. And I do some painting in the afternoons, for the craft shops. The light is wonderful then." Tourists always want to take home some splashes of colour, believing that they're supporting the local economy. They probably hang it completely incongruously on a dining room wall as a conversation piece for dinner parties before eventually deciding that it actually isn't very good and looks ridiculously out of context.

It would be several minutes, or perhaps another day, before she added: "There's Deven. He's beautiful and I've known him for years. But island men can't do proper relationships, it's not in their nature. So he comes and goes. He needs to be challenged even if he can't see it himself, then he always gets angry." She would touch the left side of her face, as though checking if it were still tender. "Men always think they possess you, don't they? You can't help getting jealous. There was that guy in Philadelphia—"

"Sorry?"

"One of the men I met online. Andy. We emailed and then we talked and I even went over there for a week. But he was just the same, kind and straight on the outside for two days but then he assumed he could do anything he liked with me. He was married, of course, I found out later. James was married too. What is it about men and honesty? He was in Rico."

"You've done some travelling, then?"

Nobody stays here if they can help it. You can't. But you keep coming back because whatever it is that brought you here is still out there.

So what was it that brought the Englishman back to this table every day? He slept, he swam and he watched the pelican, circling, watching the life beneath the surface, diving once then twice then disappearing out of sight. You could almost see him making mental notes, constructing his own story. He drank coffee and listened attentively before watching her arse sway gently away. And no-one seems to know where he went after that, in the green hire car. As far as I knew, he didn't speak to anyone else at the hotel and some of the people I know at other bars just said he might have a light lunch or a drink in the afternoon, always alone and always quiet. In the evenings he'd be on the terrace after dinner with a laptop, pausing every so often to stare out over the water as though looking for something. Still, he'd taken on some colour and he definitely looked fitter after two weeks. That's all I could tell them later.

"Hi, it's nice to see you again. Did you have a good morning?"

"Mmm."

"I was thinking, you know the island really well – the villages, the restaurants, the quiet beaches. Do you have a favourite place?" It was a little clumsy, if it was an invitation, but seemed well-meaning enough.

9

She would have noticed that but would surely ignore it. They'd been talking, in that strange way, for several days by now and this was his first attempt, or apparently so. In any case, it was surely too late.

What was it that had brought her back to sharing this table every day, to this manakin ritual dance of attention-seeking, then several small steps back? The bird is polygynous, after all. Maybe it was just simple curiosity, since a man who listened without asking anything for himself was certainly curious. Or did she have some intuition about a turning point in the undercurrent, a new direction at last, a way out? Her experiences (if we are to believe what she said) didn't suggest any great intuition. But maybe it wasn't too late.

"I have to get out of this place sometimes. I need to recover. Be myself. Nobody really knows who I am. Yes, there's a small island just to the west, almost uninhabited. You can take a small boat over and walk for hours without seeing anybody. There's a deserted beach, just the anoles, the pelican, a few petrels. Nobody knows you there. Nobody notices you. Nobody talks to you." I swear it was the first time since their meeting that she'd used the word 'you', although it still referred to herself. Nonetheless, it was still the nearest thing he'd had to an answer, so it had to mean something. And you couldn't help noticing that he'd become more alert, sitting forward in his seat with his hands inched a little closer to her though still carefully clasped.

"I understand. I think we all have a particular place we need to go. Something, or someone, gets under our skin and won't let go. Like a parasite. We live with it for a while as best we can, tell ourselves that that's just the way things are in nature, but in the end we know it can't be allowed to carry on surviving there. It's something foreign. Yet we've got used to it, it's there every day and it's even becoming part of who we are. And we can't imagine getting up tomorrow morning without it."

I'd edged a bit nearer, still with my back turned, fascinated, because this was probably the most he'd said all at one go since arriving. Nor was it exactly small talk, he'd just dived in with the psychology. And he hadn't finished.

"So many people just allow themselves to go on being abused by this thing, because it's become normal – no, it's more than that, they've let it be part of their psyche and they even welcome it. And if one day they don't feel it there, they look for it because they can't believe in a life without it. They even think of it as a sort of friend, because no-one wants to be alone. Being yourself can be lonely. But it's still a parasite." He'd paused and looked right into her eyes. "I think it takes great courage to know that, and even more to decide that you have to do something about it. It's a great strength to go away, to get out of your normal life and find that special place, a favourite place you need to go to, where you can do... well, whatever it takes to destroy that thing inside."

She'd stared at him, genuinely taken aback, then laughed out loud. But he'd simply sat back in his chair again, crossing one leg over the other in a mirror image of hers, completely unperturbed. Yes, a very calm man, within himself.

"You sound just like Michael."

"Who is Michael?"

"Some guy I talk to online. English, or Swedish, I don't remember. There've been a few weirdos. He writes stuff like that, says we need to follow a spiritual path, or something. Have to find – what was it? – our authentic self, whatever that means. We have to risk ourselves. I opened up to him about... well, about how I need to give love but no-one can be trusted. No-one. And he just writes back stuff like that. He doesn't get it."

"That's a shame."

He didn't come back the next day. Holidays always have to come to an end, I suppose, and tourists return to their lives of contrast. When she came, walking gracefully from the car in the light morning rain, the soft chenille clinging to her breasts and thighs, she'd sat alone and seemed withdrawn. She didn't touch her croissant and became edgy, shifting her position, unable to help herself turning from time to time to gaze along the beach. Her coffee went cold. Her fingers tapped the table impatiently. But he didn't come and it seemed to be eating away at her inside. After maybe half an hour she looked angry and crushed the whole pastry into fragments with a fist.

Everything comes to an end, if you're able to wait long enough. Eventually she'd got up, forgetting to pay, strode away to her car and left, wheels spinning dust. But it soon settled. And I didn't see her again.

It was almost a week later that the news reached us. The beautiful body had been found by some walkers among the rocks at the edge of a deserted beach on the small island to the west. It was naked and battered by the waves, her head crushed. Nobody had known she was there. Nobody had noticed. It was probably an accident, a rock fall. These things happen, I suppose. Although the odd thing was that they never found her clothes, and the boat was drifting out at sea.

Accidents are not good for bar trade. My part of the beach some- how seems a little emptier now, though others always arrive to fill up the spaces in time. They always like to swim in the clean blue water and then stand watching the frigates and panbirds. And of course they're always mesmerised by the diving pelican. They probably don't realise – well, hardly anyone knows it – that pelicans very rarely die of old age but of malnutrition. All that skilful diving under water to catch their prey damages their eyes, so after a while they can't see what they need. The very talent that nourishes them also, as it turns out, kills them.

The Cause of Everything

I want to tell you about this night at the Edge. It's always a weird place, even in daylight it sort of folds round you when you enter it and there's a mist rising off the streams that begin as trickles out of cracks in the higher rocks and lots of insects with long wings stroking about on little eddies of wind that follow the lines of the hill. Trees cling onto the slopes everywhere, mostly birch with their flaky white bark glowing eerie at night. It isn't even easy to walk about 'cause the hill is steep and there aren't many paths and anyway most of them end in piles of rocks or mud where the streams cross. Some parts of the place are fenced off too 'cause of old mine shafts. There's a cave just near there too, though most people don't know about it. It's low down and only about two or three feet across and you have to pull back the bushes. Even then it's just a black musty emptiness in the crumbling earth you can't see the end of.

I've always loved the place since I was a kid, which is odd 'cause for a long time I was nervous of the dark. There's a small coppice near the end of our estate, full of shadows that seem to have fingers that follow you and grab at you as you tear round on your bike, bumping over the ruts and scratching your legs on bushes 'til you're out in the sun again with heart thumping. I only joined in with the other lads 'cause, well, you have to when you're a kid or you get called names. And coming home from football practice at school in the late evenings on my own I hated crossing the park and kept wondering what was going to jump out at me.

But the Edge has always been different for me. Maybe that's 'cause there aren't any houses and people nearby – I only ever go during the week to avoid the weekend trippers – so it just feels natural. I was never even spooked by old Jeth's stories about the wizard who lives underground and how his spells light up the sky with orange and purple and how he cured the plague centuries ago in the village down the lane and has space visitors who hover over the trees in their silver machines and turn invisible when they land in the clearing. Jeth was about a hundred and eighty. Most days you'd see him mooching down our street then sitting on a bench near the playground and I'd sit with him and listen to him for ages. He used to be a woodsman, he said, 'til the National Trust took over and started fencing things off. It's always the best places that are supposed to be dangerous.

'Course, later on I got to know about how that glow in the sky is something to do with the copper or tin in the mine and the clearing is the beak of a tor, which accounts for how the trees bend over like animals bowing on their hind legs. I love those trees most of all even if they are weird. One time I'd been climbing about in them after school and stretching out along the branches feeling like I could get right inside, and maybe I fell asleep with all the effort of being a tree 'cause suddenly I jerked awake, all cold and clammy in the dark. 'Least, I think I was awake only I can't be sure now but I swear I saw some sort of silvery green shape up above me, maybe like a big otter, zigging up and down around the branches then stopping dead and disappearing like it realised I was watching and wanted me to think I hadn't seen it. I got home fast that night. Naturally, I got balled out by my mother for being late and worrying her and not having a coat on, so I never told her about it.

The only other person I've ever told was Angie. She's all right for a girl. We kind of grew up together 'cause she lives not far away and we were in the same form at school for a while and her parents used to come over and play cards with mine so we'd hang out. I think we all went on holiday together once, to Wales, and it rained for a week. Angie was good at history and that sort of stuff while I was better at maths so we helped each other with homework. She was really skinny when she was a kid like a pile of matchsticks and she had this long, straight black hair that was always falling over her face and getting in her food at lunch so then she'd swear and say she was going to get it cut. I told her not to 'cause it was funny and I liked it.

Sometimes she sat with me listening to Jeth and maybe that's why when we were alone one day I told her about the thing in the trees. 'Course then she insisted on coming with me and wouldn't take no for an answer so it wasn't my private place anymore. She loved it too, specially when I showed her where you could get through the fence and peer into the cave. Then she'd say stupid stuff like she could hear the wizard's kettle boiling so we should go down and have some tea, you know, teasing me. But she was all right, I didn't mind, I liked being with her. She even said that lots of other people had seen the zigging green things and most of them hadn't just woken up from trying to be a tree and she'd heard her parents talking – you know, like grown-ups do in low voices when they think you've gone to bed – about some man at the university who's been studying it and has a theory so probably I'm not completely mad.

Naturally, her parents told her to keep away from the Edge. And they weren't too sure about me, either. Maybe all that was really 'cause of some kid who went missing a while ago. I read about it one Saturday afternoon when my mother had given me some money for the cinema – she had a bunch of other women coming round for something or other – but I didn't fancy that so I got a burger instead and had a sly ciggie in a coffee bar where the guy who owned it didn't mind. Then I went to the library to look at some old newspapers. No, I'm not a nerd, it was a school history project and I thought I'd surprise Angie by finding out some stuff she didn't know.

What I found out was this local mystery, when some young kid had gone off on his own like kids do and just disappeared, then the family dog went off too and they found it sitting by the cave on the Edge and whining. Some men got inside but they didn't find anything and said it was all blocked off a little way down anyway. It reminded me of one of Jeth's stories about witches who sacrificed children some-where around here, only I'm pretty sure he made that one up. Nobody really knows. Like I said, kids are always wandering off and doing stuff they're not supposed to.

Well, back to the point. This particular night it's summer and I'm fifteen. It's Angie's birthday the next day so we've gone up to the Edge for a sort of early party, just us. It wasn't much of a spread, to be honest. In our larder I'd found a big bag of crisps and a packet of those long iced cakes she likes even if her hair does always get stuck in them and I sneaked out a bottle of wine that was already opened but nearly half full. Perhaps I should have made more of an effort, thinking about it. Both our folks had gone out to some meeting on the other side of town and said they'd be back late so we're supposed to go to the cinema. That's always where we're supposed to go when they don't want us at home, only we didn't finish homework until after eight and neither of us were interested in the films showing.

Woodland

We're sitting up on the small sandy clearing that's almost the highest point and Jeth once said was right above the wizard's tomb. I hadn't swallowed that one 'cause wizards aren't supposed to die, are they, and if he was dead then how could he still do those colour spells and have aliens visiting? It's still quite light and you can see down below how the hills roll away for miles through a few ruined stone buildings that must have been part of some old village before the spacecraft flattened it. We're feeling really high up. Over on one side you can just see the corner of one of the long flat buildings of the research station through the trees. I don't know what they research there and Angie said it was biology or something like that.

We're in a crazy mood talking about Jeth's old stories and wondering whether the wiz is really stretched out a few feet down and maybe only sleeping after all. Perhaps some silvery-green things will come zigging down to join us 'cause they liked buns and Angie's giggling and says she hopes that nobody ever finds out the truth. The wine might have been having an effect on us too only as it starts getting darker the Edge feels more weird than usual with no moon yet and the place is absolutely quiet so we start whispering too.

It's like the Edge is just hanging around us now like when you're wrapped up in a blanket with just your eyes peering out. And we aren't cold at all but still Angie shifts herself over close to me and we share a ciggie even though I've never seen her have one before, she always said it was stupid. She seems somehow different to usual tonight and we're both getting that feeling of magic about the place. I remember that specially 'cause most of the time we get all caught up in normal things like school and football and what's for dinner, but then there are some moments when suddenly you feel out of it all. You can never see them coming. It feels like you don't belong in the world after all – or maybe you do but the world isn't what you thought it was. I'm not sure I can explain it. It's just that occasionally you get a special moment and they're the best of all and nothing to be frightened of even if you are spaced out 'cause they mean, I don't know, that life isn't all ordinary. You don't have to understand it.

So then she puts her head on my shoulder and I can smell her hair all fresh and feel it falling down my neck so I put my arm around her like you automatically do when someone's close. It's good being like that with her all soft and warm and I realise she isn't skinny anymore and I could probably stay like this for hours, relaxed and quiet as we watch the light fade and the stars come out. But then she moves even closer and lifts her head and kisses me on the mouth. It's the first time we've done that and it goes on for ages until I start feeling hot and a bit confused. The inside of my head is spinning too like something with flashing lights is circling round and coming in to land and sure enough I can't see anything.

To tell the truth I'm feeling awkward 'cause where we're sitting is on a bit of a slope and I have to put one arm down to keep myself steady only it's shaking like it doesn't want to be mine anymore and Angie is pressing my lips so hard I can't help falling back. Then she reaches over and takes my other hand and puts it on her shirt and holds it there so I can feel her breast. 'Course that's the first time too and now both our hearts are thumping like they're racing each other. Next thing is we've rolled over on our sides and there are legs everywhere and somehow a couple of her buttons have come loose and my hand is inside touching her.

That seems to make her feel shy and she says to stop though she doesn't do the buttons up again. So we sit there for a while wondering what to think with all this energy still zigging about until suddenly Angie stands up and says let's go for a walk. It seems like a good enough idea even if my legs aren't very steady but we're still in this funny mood and soon we're getting through the fence at the secret place I told you about and heading for the cave.

I know it was daft, you don't have to tell me, going exploring when it's almost dark and telling each other it's about time we found out the truth about the wizard and what he can really do. I mean, how many times have we been here before and not bothered because it's all just stories, so why now? Then, thinking about it, maybe that's exactly it – we knew the place so well after all this time that we aren't frightened or anything and even though it gets so quiet at night and the spaces between the trees fill up with dark purple shadows I never really think these days about ghosts and witches and stuff. And even if the wizard is real and isn't dead he must be a kind chap who'll invite us in for tea because he cured plagues, didn't he?

Anyway, nothing would've stopped Angie now. She's got this wild side to her and even though she's too smart to ever get into trouble it just leaks out sometimes and you couldn't stop her if you wanted to. I can see it. 'Course, she always knows how to get away with things like when she dared me to bunk off a couple of times and we hid our school things and got a bus into the city, just mooching about. No-one ever found out or did anything about it. Me, I was always looking over my shoulder but she can be very persuasive.

She's making me go first now and telling me what to do. After you get through the fence and over a few rocks the easiest thing to do is walk right across the clearing only now she says we have to be slow and quiet so here I am creeping through the trees and the long grass that always seems to be wet even in summer. She says we mustn't leave a trace anywhere only I can't see that anyone could have known anyway.

I pull back a couple of the bushes and feel inside but I can't see anything and it smells odd too, not bad but something I can't quite make out. I'm still shaking a bit but we're here now and I suppose part of me has always wanted to do it so when Angie gives me a bit of a push I get down on my knees and ease myself through. It slopes down a bit inside so I slither onto some sort of ledge and I'm surprised that it's not all blocked off like the men said when they were looking for the kid, in fact it's bigger on the inside than you'd think. My eyes start getting used to the darkness and actually there are sort of sparks of light

20

reflecting off water trickling down the walls so I see that I can jump down and stand up quite easily. Angie is coming too right behind me and then she's next to me with a big smile and her face close to mine and the long black hair curling round us. Looking back I can just make out some of the trees and the dark sky past the entrance but we aren't going back now 'cause we're completely alone in our own private world and wondering why we haven't done this before.

I'm not sure about everything that happened after this 'cause I wasn't seeing things clearly, I mean like normal. I've never been in a place like this before and it feels a bit like dreaming – you know how you're never sure whether a dream lasts as long as it seems or only a few seconds and when you wake up and remember it some of the things that happened are actually impossible? It was like that.

The cave turns out not to be very long after all and I'm pretty disappointed at first even though Angie says she can hear the kettle boiling, but I kiss her anyway and say there has to be more to it than this or it wouldn't be worthwhile for those aliens to make the trip, and she laughs at that. Then we start loping around in big silly steps like we're on the moon and tapping on the rock for a secret switch or something. And in a funny sort of way I find one, at least some stones come loose and when I move them a draught comes through and makes us both shiver. So then we both start pulling away hard at them and pretty soon there's a gap you can see through and there's another cave there. We're really excited now and tearing at the stones with our bare hands and not caring that our clothes are getting messed up and our arms scratched. Angie has some blood on her shirt too and all the buttons have come loose so I can see her bra and her white skin but she doesn't seem to mind. When the hole's big enough I crawl through first and then help her 'cause there's quite a big drop on the other side so I'm holding her around the legs while she slides down and now my hands are under her skirt almost up to her waist. I want to apologise or something 'cause I've never touched her like that but she's just beaming like a cat so I don't say anything.

It's still sparking off the walls and we can see a tunnel just ahead of us, pretty low but not so you have to bend over much and it goes on sloping down for ages and definitely getting warmer too until it opens out into this fantastic long cave with a stream rushing along through it. There are lots of points of light shining in the rock here and I say we must be near the mine and they're pieces of metal or crystals or something like that. Anyway we can see our way pretty easily which seems weird considering how far we've come. Angie says this must be the wizard's entrance hall and any moment now a dwarf dressed like a penguin will appear to take our hats and coats if we had any. She's enjoying it all, maybe even more excited than me. Like I say, she can be wild. Well, there aren't any dwarves so we carry on by ourselves.

The sound of the water is getting louder now, and then... well, it still makes me shudder to think about it, only the cave just opens out into the most incredible sight and all I can say is I can't move with the shock. There's water pouring down from somewhere up near the roof and it's bouncing off all the rocks with spray flashing all around us and somehow making the place light up even more. The noise is almost deafening and the air's really fresh too.

I turn and shout something to Angie but she isn't next to me anymore and then I see her clambering down to this big deep pool where the water's swirling around before disappearing off down another tunnel. The spray is zigging all around her and breaking up the light into purple and blue and yellow flashes and she's laughing and taking off her clothes and dancing about under it, waving at me to come down. But I still can't move even more now.

Well, you've probably never heard Angie laugh but it gets inside your head and then you'll do anything she says. So I stop being amazed and forget about where we are and when we're supposed to be home and in a minute I'm there with her both playing about like kids with our skin soaked through. And I'm just thinking this can go on forever when she comes right up to me with her face shining and her hair sticking all over it and she puts her arms round my neck so her whole body is pressed against me. And then just as suddenly she decides she's had enough and is climbing out, grabbing our clothes and pulling me behind her by the hand and heading for another tunnel. I'm following her like a slave or like there's nothing else I can do now but go along wherever and I'm thinking that maybe this is exactly what the wizard's home should be like after all.

After this, things start getting really eerie. There are different tunnels to choose between and after you go a little way down one it splits again and Angie is making me choose. I'm hesitating and I keep thinking which way is north but to tell the truth I've lost track ages ago and I couldn't've even found the way back where we've come from so there's nothing for it but to guess and keep going. Another thing is we're getting further and further away from the big cave and it's getting colder and darker. I'm glad I'm with Angie 'cause anyone else might've lost their nerve, but in a funny way we're enjoying being completely lost and being together.

When we hit the mine shaft it's quite a shock, I can tell you. I say we can't possibly be there unless we've gone round in a big circle but she says maybe it's another one we didn't know about before. At least the air is fresher here but we're on a narrow ledge and then something scuttles away around our feet making us jump. Now Angie is getting nervous one minute and excited the next then crying a bit until I don't know what to make of it or what to say. But I know I have to do something.

I can just make out some sort of panel on the wall not far from my head so I sidle over and hit a button. We both jump again when suddenly cables we haven't seen start moving with a creaking noise from down below like a lift coming up. Angie looks at me with her eyes big and round and asking me all sorts of things I can't answer, then she buries her face in my neck and holds on tight to me. And when the lift arrives we just get in, like you do, and I push another button to go up but I'm not even that surprised when it starts going the other way. Trouble is, it's getting faster and faster and we try some of the other buttons but there's nothing we can do to stop it. The noise all around us from the cables is deafening along with the air rushing up like it's escaping from wherever we're going and somewhere nearby we can hear water, I mean, a lot of it. This is definitely no time for wizard jokes.

We hit the bottom and scream into each other's faces as we fall out locked together like there's only one of us. And here's the water, tons of it racing past and roaring at us 'cause we're in it now and disappearing into some huge shadow. I can hardly think anymore but I make a grab for a rock jutting out from the side with one arm while the other's holding onto Angie as tight as I can, but I swear the rock shrieks and runs away and I can see bones behind where it was like a skinny skeleton. Angie's still crying and laughing all at the same time and holding onto me so hard it hurts.

And just as I'm thinking what kind of wizard lives here, the water's gone chasing itself down the hill and we're thrown into the air and find ourselves rolling over each other on the long wet grass at the bottom of the Edge, laughing our heads off.

So now we're lying on our backs looking up at the stars and it's completely silent again. I turn my head to look at Angie. Her hair is a deep purple between the trees and small sandy hills are shining in the moonlight as the dark forest rises and falls slowly with each breath of the earth. And I know that if she can do this magic there's nothing for me but to follow her wherever she wants to go.

Holy Sh!t

1 Good Friday

Marcus steps out onto the patio and lifts the Glencairn crystal glass to his lips. There is a moment of pure gold splashed along the third finger of his right hand as the late afternoon September sun catches the single malt, but he misses it. The other hand thrust deep into a pocket of his dark business suit, red Italian silk tie pulled loose and hanging over one shoulder, he stands with legs apart and glares out across the long garden towards the hazel copse beyond, alive with starlings discussing their day.

"For Chrissake," he swears softly to himself, "the countryside's supposed to be peaceful. You spend your week in the concrete and pay your million to get away from it on Friday, and when you get home you can't fucking hear yourself think."

Marcus Boyd is normally a calm man and would never speak like this were others around. But what he thinks, and how and when he expresses it, are very different. Natural aggression and a great deal of self-belief are essential characteristics for a successful futures broker, along with the ability of a born gambler never to betray any inner disturbance. Certainly, at least by all the parameters of the City, he is successful and there should be no need to work given another two or three years. (Although, it recently crossed his mind briefly, what does a wealthy man do at forty-five, at the height of reason but without work?)

It has been a good week. True, there was a moment today when the whole floor had held its breath and even the screens seemed to hesitate, casting questioning glances at one another as African grains wobbled. But the people who mattered held their nerve and the next bonus was secure. Solomon even shot him half a relieved smile and a pat on the shoulder as he left. Marcus has been on a high and for the whole forty-five minutes on the train out of Waterloo plus the fifteen walking from the station he thought of little else but sitting in his quiet garden with a whisky, telling his wife how clever he is.

But Beth isn't home and the murmuration overhead is getting bigger by the minute, arriving in tens and twenties with excited chattering and flapping wings. Driven by numbers, Marcus wanders down the offset York stone path, eyes concentrated, trying to count them. Halfway along and no more than two feet to his right, the colony of tiny red ants pauses for a moment as he passes before continuing its work of sucking all the goodness from the soil and ruining the immaculate stripe of the newly-mown lawn.

He vaguely remembers their gardener, Tom, telling him one day that starlings can be vicious, invading others' territories and evicting even stronger nesting birds. Tom would also have said, had he been asked, and because his life was rooted in the land, that outbreaks of red ants represent hidden, unresolved anger.

When Beth comes in she tosses her keys into the Chinese hand-painted blue porcelain flower vase on the hall table and kicks off her shoes, leaving them where they fall as she shakes her head to get school out of it.

"My God, you wouldn't believe how stupid highly educated people can be," she calls out, letting go the frustration. "The honourable staffroom treasurer says we have plenty of money in the bank but he still wants a twenty-five per cent increase in our subs because ten pounds is a nice round figure and easier to collect. And they all voted for it. Can you imagine? Sorry I'm late. Staff meeting. Marc?"

He can't hear her of course and he's nowhere to be seen. You spend your week trying to knock education into over-privileged kids who don't want it – and, let's face it, probably don't need it given their family connections – with petty colleagues who won't co-operate and all you want to do on a Friday is sit in your garden with a glass of Sauvignon and tell your husband that really you love it because even if it's part-time it's worthwhile and important for your self-respect. She pours the wine anyway and takes it upstairs.

Under the soft, warm shower she imagines it's champagne and begins to feel a little better as the water wipes tension out of her muscles and washes away the dust of other people. She doesn't move for five minutes. Then she takes the gel and gently rubs the creamy lather along her thighs, up and around in practised circular stokes across her taut abdomen and around each breast in turn, probing with a careful finger as one instinctively does at this age.

Leaving the shower on, she steps out for a moment to stand silently with towel in hand before the full length mirror, the school week over, a woman at home, thinking that life's not in bad shape after all. She has all she needs, more than enough in fact, and she still has hopes for the future. But then... there is something. A presence. A hidden door in her mind is on the point of opening, and for some reason she's a little fearful of what lies beyond it. Beth frowns, and a brief cold shadow races across her wet skin as a flock of birds at the end of the garden rises as one dark being and takes off across the face of the early evening sun.

Marcus feels it too, despite the peace that has finally descended in their stead. The earlier mood of elation and self-satisfaction has all but evaporated and he is annoyed with himself for letting something so transitory get to him. The thing is, really, this disturbance was something he could do nothing about, there being no algorithm with which to control birds. Unlike ants. Here was a situation he could intervene. He notices them immediately as he walks slowly back towards the house. He's proud of this garden, its shapes and forms – especially its size and the fact that he owns it – and he knows every line of it. These creatures cannot be allowed to despoil that and are summarily dealt with, the nest penetrated several times with a sharp stick and blanketed thoroughly with the white powder.

Tom would say that this only delays the inevitable, since there are so many of them by now and they have spread beneath the surface.

Washing his hands in the kitchen, from nowhere comes suddenly the irresistible urge for a cigarette. He'd given up as a fortieth birthday present to himself. Another achievement, an assertion of control. But what the hell, he has earned the right to make his own decisions and accept the consequences. He searches the kitchen and finds Beth's handbag, for some reason on top of the fridge, so Marcus opens it to get her packet. What he also finds is a CD, with no jewel case but with the letters H S scrawled with blue marker pen on a sticky label.

"What's—?" he begins but as he walks into the hallway he hears the running water upstairs and realises she can't hear him.

He might as well take a look at it, since they have no secrets from each other. It is an intrigue, after all. Beth is an artist – that is to say, she had pretensions of being an artist twenty-odd years ago when they'd met as students, had realised its pointlessness and become a teacher instead – and is yet to embrace the twentieth century culturally let alone the new millennium. Marcus knows no-one less likely to carry a casual CD in their handbag, except perhaps his own mother although you take it for granted when eighty year-olds do strange things.

So he pours another single malt and settles down at a desk in his study, idly pushing the mouse around as a jumble of filenames come and go on the screen. It's just some amateur home-made game. You are the chief of some remote village and each season you have to decide how many of your people to deploy in various tasks, such as cultivating the fields, going out on fishing expeditions, repairing houses and boats, guarding against enemy attacks and so on. Then the program chooses the weather conditions and strength of your enemies – is this random, he wonders? – tells you how much food you've gathered in the season and how many people you've lost.

Marcus spends his week studying data and betting on their future so, with nothing else to do right now, he tosses in some figures and feels personally affronted a few minutes later to learn that his population has been decimated, as much by raiders as by rainfall. With so many young men lost the birth rate has fallen too and his village is on the verge of extinction. He is left with a choice between starvation and slavery.

Beth comes downstairs, changed and refreshed, moves straight to the fridge for her cigarettes, frowns, pours another glass of wine and eventually locates her handbag next to the toaster. It doesn't entirely surprise her to find it open. Marcus is that kind of man. They had after all promised to love and obey and endow each other with all their worldly goods, and he was a literal kind of man, especially since he'd done most the endowing. So what's hers is his too. She smiles to herself, obediently, at the irony that he still won't let her near the keys of the Audi.

She takes the lasagne out to defrost and starts washing the salad, looking out as she loves to do from the sink across the length of the beautiful garden, feeling the harmony of its natural palette and the grace of… but there's a white patch near the path, halfway down. A disturbance. A key begins to turn on the inner lock. Beth calls out for Marcus to get ready, prepare the table and put chairs out on the patio, but the study door's closed. They've been home together nearly an hour now and neither has seen nor heard the other.

"You're going to be late," she says gently, breaking the spell, putting her arms around his neck and resting a cheek on his hair. His intense glare reflects back at her from the screen and he says nothing, calculating mentally. "They'll be here at eight and you haven't even changed yet."

"Who will?" he murmurs absently without taking his eyes from the screen.

"Andy Davidson, from school. With his sister, I did tell—"

"Where did you get this thing? It was in your bag."

For the first time she notices what he's looking at instead of his reflection. The graphics are fairly crude and the colours mostly primary but it's recognisably the plan of a settlement between water and forest divided into tessellating geometric figures. As they watch, a small dark cloud spreads slowly from the trees, swallowing up groups of little stick men before just as slowly receding and disappearing.

"Are you dead yet?" she laughs.

"It's not funny," he snaps. "You think you know what's going on then something different happens. There don't seem to be any proper rules. I was on top of it five minutes ago, plenty of food, breeding like rabbits, all set to expand. Then this starts happening. It doesn't make sense."

"Well, lie down and die with dignity," she suggests, straightening up, "then go and have a shower. And if you don't open the wine soon it won't breathe, as you keep telling me. And we don't want the wine to be dead too, do we?" She leaves him, to prepare the table herself.

"Have you thought what you'd like for you birthday yet?" she calls out over her shoulder from the next room. "It's only a week now, you haven't said."

He doesn't say.

The dinner party doesn't start well. Marcus isn't ready and nor is the claret. Andrew is a quiet, serious young man barely more than half Beth's age and while they've struck up an easy friendship at school on the mathematics of natural perspective and the artfulness of mathematics, the social dynamics of a staffroom do not translate easily to the Surrey countryside. There is suddenly an acute, if unspoken, awareness of the obvious differences between them that seem heavily to outweigh their shared interests. They come from different worlds, inhabiting different attitudes. For perhaps the first time, Beth feels self-conscious about her lifestyle and the things she takes for granted. She also feels her age.

And if Andrew, even in a pale suit and white shirt, is of a different species then his sister is truly alien. Older than him in her early thirties, Mary is tall and painfully slim, with stunning dark eyes that hardly seem to move yet take in every detail around her. Shining blonde hair falls loosely over bare shoulders. A thin, simple white dress conceals little. Worst of all is her unearthly calm, as one who has been through the most raging storms unscathed, or perhaps several lifetimes. The door of awareness swings open as Beth realises that the arrival of this creature will change everything.

While they wait for Marcus, they walk in the garden. It has always impressed people, the happily colourful borders, the smooth curves and private areas separated off by shrubs and entered beneath rose arches, the rockeries of pale grey Lakeland stone, then the sweep of lawn down to the wood beyond. But tonight the lines seem like tracks, the borders a stiff jacket, the stones cold. Despite the pleasure she always feels when entertaining, Beth fights her inner deflation and leads them back to the patio chairs where they laugh lightly about the staff meeting, murmur private information about certain recalcitrant pupils and wait awkwardly for the main character to make his entrance.

31

He does so some fifteen minutes after eight with a gruff apology and a clear air of distraction, unspokenly put down to a difficult day of business. It could hardly be mentioned that this week Marcus has earned more than Andrew's annual salary. He gestures vaguely with one hand as he sits.

"You like the garden?" It is more a statement of evident fact than a question. "We have a man twice a week. A genius, our Tom."

"It's very... organised."

Mary's voice is soft, far deeper than one might expect, and very clear as though each word has been instantaneously weighed among a hundred others before deliberate selection for its task. Marcus senses the challenge and looks up, eyebrows raised, from pouring the wine. He recovers himself quickly but nonetheless his watching wife sees the dilation of his pupils as he notices, and scans, the younger woman for the first time. A man cannot help this.

"You mean it's Home Counties, over-cultivated, no wilderness? But isn't that why we have gardens, to free ourselves from the wild?" Oh my God, Beth is thinking already, these two can read one another's thoughts and neither of them much likes what they read.

"And there's no water," Mary adds simply.

"Oh, you can't keep fish here," Beth jumps in to try and lighten the exchange. "Herons you see. Or the feral cats get them." She bites her lip, berating herself for sounding ridiculous.

"Still—" Andrew tries. He's less sensitive but he does know his sister well and can recognise certain signs. "—it is very peaceful, especially after the City, I expect."

"You wouldn't think that," Marcus grumbles, "if you'd been here when I got home. An awful din, the birds over the copse down there. More than five hundred at an estimate, dark grey things, well, sort of speckled with green and purple. Couldn't hear yourself think. Off on their holidays to the sun by now, I suppose."

32

"Starlings, dear," Beth brightens, on safer ground now. "And they would have been arriving, not leaving. They come here for the winter." Marcus sits back and smiles at her with a hint of mockery around his eyes.

"And how on Earth did you know that?"

"Oh, you know, I just do. Probably learned it when I was a girl, like recognising trees or knowing one flower from another." And, she observes silently, when one is married to a man like you it's important to have control over a few things even if it's just the names of birds, the ingredients of a lasagne or the timing of a fake orgasm.

"I really admire that," says Mary. Beth starts slightly, fearing that she's read that last thought too. "I mean, naming the things around us. We really should know what we're each a part of, what we're living alongside. How else can we really know ourselves—" the word is stressed "—and our place in the world? These things help us to know why we're here, don't they?"

Marcus grunts but keeps his thoughts hidden out of practised courtesy toward guests and business rivals. Some of us know ourselves quite well enough, thank you. Some of us aren't doing too badly even without being able to name more than three birds. Some of us, thank heavens, have a grasp of reality and don't need to be told why we're here. Some of us might have nice tits but they don't stop us having cotton wool between our ears and no idea how to make a good living.

"You're inspiring me, Beth," continues Mary. "Now that I'm back in England, I'm going to learn all those things. Really I will. Come on, you can start teaching me while I help you with the dinner."

There's an uneasy pause after the two women go indoors, a certain serrated atmosphere trailing after them. It is down to Marcus, the senior male here, to move things on.

"Well, an interesting girl, your sister. A bit of a hippy. Did she say she's been abroad? What was it, Kathmandu, some barmy ashram?"

"Only briefly, I think," Andrew answers, staring with fierce intensity into the middle distance and hoping to hide there. "Most of the time she's been in Timor-Leste. About five years. She's a specialist in tropical diseases… malaria and stuff. Er, a doctor."

II   Acts of Gods

As they sit down to their meagre meal in the dust beside the wooden cabin, Uc!ram breaks the bread and quietly voices the prayer of grace but with hardly a grain of conviction. Sitting opposite him, his wife loyally bows her head and repeats the words but watches anxiously, from the corner of one eye, his spirit disintegrate as surely as the food between his fingers. She reaches out a hand to console him but he pulls away.

"I'm sorry Lies!a, I cannot do this. I am not worthy of our people, or of you. And I am no longer worthy of the priesthood."

"Uc!ram, please—" Her gentle voice does little to soften the guttural name.

"No. If nothing else, the gods have taught me that in dishonesty there is certain eternal death. And if I, Uc!ram the priest, cannot face the truth – that I have failed – then we are all lost."

"Ha!" They are both shaken from their mournfulness by the sarcastic exclamation, not noticing the young man's approach. "We're lost anyway, old man. How can you even sit there with your bread and your fine wife and fine cabin while all around you your people die?" He gestures towards the bare earth of the clearing below the hill, dotted with small groups of silent figures sitting in threadbare clothes beside clay huts.

"Who cares about your kind of truth now?" Ad!yn continues. "The boats are wrecked by storms and there's no-one to repair them. Most of our young men, my friends, are drowned or murdered. Mothers sit before us with no sons. Husbands sit with no wives, carried off by exhaustion from working rock-hard fields or by disease or by our enemies, to be enslaved – or worse. There is not enough food for another season and—"

"Do you think I don't know all this?" Uc!ram responds angrily, getting to his feet and standing face to face with the other, who steps back with instinctive deference. Ageing, yes, and with back a little bent now, nevertheless he is a powerful man and still holds authority. "Do you think I am not torn by grief and confusion every minute of the day, seeing what is happening to these people I love? Knowing that I am responsible?"

"That's right, you are responsible," counters Ad!yn, recovering his boldness and renewing the challenge. "It's your job to commune with the gods and learn what is to be. We trusted you when you told us how many were to stand guard, what to sow in the fields, when to set out on the waters."

"How could anyone imagine this would happen?" Lies!a jumps to her husband's defence, forgetting, in the heat of their pain, her duty of silence when men dispute. She points to the devastation evident at every turn. "There has never been a storm like that, the very sky lit up by fire. We have never seen before those flying creatures, those... we don't even have a name for them, the things that devour our crops. And the Am!der have never in memory attacked from the north. This... this chaos is the work of some new devil."

Uc!ram tries to quieten her but she will not be stopped, her eyes spitting anger at the usurper. "And are you so very young, Ad!yn, that you forget how good life was just a few seasons ago, when the stores overflowed and we built new boats and the evenings rang out with the laughter of children and the songs of the young women and—" She stops abruptly, a hand to her mouth as though trying to take back the words. Ad!yn's sister had been killed in the last attack.

"I don't forget," the young man hisses, barely holding himself back from striking out. Even in these circumstances that would be unforgivable and, however just his argument, he would have lost it. There are rules, within the tribe as within the family, handed down through all the generations before a child could even walk and the breaking of these would signal the end of time itself. There is a tense silence as the realisation grows in the collective mind that the turning point has been reached.

"So what went wrong, priest?" Ad!yn continues, now with the calmness of one who knows his time is coming. "Did you forget how to talk to the gods? Did they begin to speak a different language perhaps? Well, if you don't learn it very fast, someone else must try in your place."

Darkness falls and with it an unseasonal chill descends on the village, forcing the seventy or so wretched souls inside their huts to wrap themselves in the wool of sheep and goats that no longer graze the hillsides. Lies!a has stayed where she was, in the dust, weeping quietly for the suffering people and their tortured leader, her husband. He is a good man who has grown in wisdom and understanding through many seasons of observing the traditions, of meditation and communion with the spirits on the mountain, of learning to cast the stones, to read signs and stars. He had been the obvious and worthy successor to her father. And it is true that they have known many seasons of peace and plenty with his guidance.

Of course there have been unforeseen disasters from time to time, stronger floods than usual, new strains of illness, untimely attacks. There have been losses. But the people accept these as the natural flow of things, as winter follows summer, as death is a part of life. It has always been in balance. They have always recovered because Uc!ram is a cautious leader who stores up reserves and strength in good times and holds the younger ones back when their enthusiasm would rush them into danger. And the people accept that his knowledge cannot be perfect; he may (it is assumed) talk with the gods, but he is not a god. Nor is he a gambler.

All the same, everything that was said earlier, however cruel, was true. They have been ravaged by disharmony beyond imagination and the very seasons seem to have lost their natural rhythm. All the rules have somehow changed. Perhaps the gods have indeed staked them in a game of dice, and lost. In any case, Uc!ram has lost. Perhaps – she shudders at the outrage of her own thought – it is indeed time for him to let go.

High above her to the east, as the twin moons rise over the forest, the priest sits quietly before the altar just beneath the mountain peak and has the same thought. He has been praying these two hours. He has cut his flesh with a sharp rock and lain prostrate and naked before the fire, offering his own blood to the holy cup. He has cast the stones.

And he hasn't the faintest idea what the gods are saying to him.

III Playing the Game

"What was that you were saying earlier about a game?" Mary asks. The meal has passed off well enough, most sensitive subjects being skilfully avoided, and they are sitting on the patio with coffee. The evening is drawing itself together as the first stars dimly appear, and it is just warm enough beneath the canopy to enjoy a quiet hour, nature having apparently already gone to bed.

Marcus looks across at her, brandy to his lips, and hesitates before replying as if calculating the motive behind her question. There is always a reason and he admits to himself that this is a disturbing young woman. She has refused his excellent claret and drunk only mineral water. She has refused to talk about her experiences abroad. What else, he couldn't help wondering, being a man, would she refuse?

"You said you were late because of a silly game," she went on. "You don't seem like a man who would do anything silly. Or play games."

"You're quite right there," agrees Beth, seeking a possible ally in this creature that she, too, is unsure of. "Not even Monopoly at Christmas anymore. Says it's too easy and—" in a mock deep voice "—'life is too serious.' No, this was just something I brought home from school. I caught one of the boys playing it instead of doing his CAD – his design – so I confiscated it. Forgot I still had it. Seems to be a bit of a craze in the Sixth Form just now. The kids call it Holy Shit, for some reason. Do you know Andy?"

"Well, I know about it, yes." He's said very little throughout the evening, that rare guest who's content to listen, smile in the right places and respond when it's necessary to prompt someone else. One who prefers others to take the lead, which has suited Marcus fine. The sort of young man who could be thought either entirely out of his depth or frighteningly intelligent and too nice to be true. The fact of the matter, Beth finds herself thinking, is that our Andrew is all of these things by turn. And a young man who can at once appeal to the mother and the woman will certainly have his day.

"It was written by a student of mine, Su-li, a Chinese girl, strange background. Rather a strange girl, actually, but very clever. I believe it was an IT project. I don't know much about programming myself but people say the game is pretty original."

"Well, I don't know about that," Marcus objects. He describes the concept in a few sentences. "Interesting enough, I suppose, but basically simplistic. I mean, there's obviously a formula programmed with a few random elements but that's security-coded. Still, it's not hard to figure out the basic strategy. For example, in summer you put more people to work in the fields, but when you've got plenty of food you can expect more attacks from other tribes. That sort of thing."

"From what I've heard," says Andrew, warming to his own subject, "it's based on Conway's Game of Life, except that that's purely logical with a limited number of fixed rules. The students were invited to make a version that's more realistic and introduce some random elements."

"What's the Game of Life? It sounds fun," asks Beth, hoping to bring the conversation down to earth but soon regretting it. Andrew takes a notebook and pen from his pocket and roughly sketches a grid of squares, putting crosses in a few of them.

"You start with a group of crosses, representing people, like this, then decide on a few rules. For example, if a cross has less than two neighbours it will die – that's called loneliness – and if it has more than three neighbours it dies of overcrowding. On the other hand, if an empty square has, say, two crosses as neighbours then a new person is born there." He sketches another grid to show how the group changes.

"Then you apply the rules again and keep going like that. There can be all sorts of strange outcomes – your group might die out completely after a while or expand and move across the grid. It's fascinating. So what Su-li did was give some of the people individual jobs, dress the rules up as weather patterns and insert some hidden consequences. She seems to have used some chaos theory too, though, which is beyond the syllabus. Like I say, she's pretty clever."

"Ah, but—" his days of Maths might be far behind him but Marcus has an ear for logic "—chaos isn't random, is it? There are formulae." He sits back with a smile of triumph, although nobody else is sure why.

"Still unpredictable, though, given unlimited variables," counters Mary quietly. "It's like epidemiology. However much we think we know about cholera, we never know exactly how it's going to spread in a population."

"Surely that's just down to the r-number, the reproduction rate?" Marcus frowns, needing to wrest back some control.

"Yes, you'd think so," agrees Mary. "But—" Oh my God, thinks Beth, this girl is not only stunning… something has to be done about her. "—even that behaves unpredictably at times. Take May's population formula. It looks straightforward enough and as r increases past two the population goes up and down naturally. But at two point six you get chaos."

"And at about two point eight," interjects Andy, "it settles down again for a little while. Very weird. No-one knows why."

Marcus might not know the numbers but he knows the markets and can read the moving averages. And the weather forecasts. Yes, odd things happen from time to time – one had happened earlier today – but then it's just a matter of keeping your nerve until the hiccup passes. Everything is based on rules, after all. He grunts and says so.

"Well, if it's all so simple, why were you on the point of extinction when I came in?" Beth teases him.

"Well, that's what I mean about this game being silly." He really isn't going to let this go, Friday evening social occasion or not. Suddenly, it seems to be a matter of pride. "Right, so I was just passing the time after I got home. Unwinding. And I'd cracked the game, my village was totally successful, bursting with people and food and expanding across the islands, when all kinds of new stuff suddenly starts happening that hasn't been mentioned before. New variables you haven't been told about. And before you know it you're worse off than when you started. Sorry, but I ask you – what sort of game is it when all the rules keep changing?"

There's an uncomfortable silence as the other three intuitively know the answer to that but don't say so, not wanting to incur the host's indignation. Beth desperately wants to change the subject. This is partly out of loyalty and to defend her husband from the challenge, since it can only go one way, and partly because she got lost several minutes earlier. What would be an appropriate link – the beauty of mathematical proportion, the inherent chaos of abstract art...? She's still trying to decide when Mary comes in for the kill.

"It's not at all silly, in fact it's brilliantly realistic," she offers, leaning forward with her chin on a palm so that the long blonde hair falls forward perfectly framing her face. "It was precisely because you were so strong, as you believed, that you became all but extinct. You went too far, over-reached. You probably tried to take over territory that wasn't yours and were out of balance with your environment. We see that all around us across the world, don't we? Being strong isn't the same as being successful, Marcus."

He grunts again and conveniently realises that the brandy is finished, excusing himself to fetch more. Beth lets out a long, silent breath of relief. The atmosphere has been becoming just a touch explosive. Her husband usually likes a challenge – that kind of masculine strength is a powerful attraction for a woman like, well, her – but he can neither bear nor excuse it if he thinks others are not playing by the rules. His rules. This evening, he seems to have met his match.

"So why do they call it Holy Shit, Andy?" she asks.

"It's real life," Mary suggested. "Horrible things happen even to good people."

"No, it's not that," Andy points out. "Its proper name is Shih-T'ai, based on some ancient Chinese philosophy."

"It still amounts to crap," Marcus observes, returning with more brandy and chilled water for Mary, "if the events are random—"

"But they're not, that's the point," protests Andy.

"—or so complicated that the player can never know what they are."

Andy gives the practised apologetic shrug of the mathematician who realises that no-one else really gives a hoot about his subject, whilst Mary, with subtle grace and inevitability, now quietly takes over.

"I bet you're just missing something, Marcus. There must be a clue somewhere to get on top of the situation."

"Don't think so. It's just mean. Well… now that you mention it, there's a little icon that appears sometimes, looks a bit like a mountain."

"There you are, then. Why don't you show me?"

Beth not only feels the lock turn inside her but senses a dark shadow rushing through the open door.

The next morning, she is still awake as the dawn rises with the chattering of the starlings, or whatever the hell they are, in the copse. Marcus stayed up late with the blessed game, inspired, determined that he knew how to beat it now, and he'd slept in the spare room. So she gets up to make coffee and walk in the garden, in her nightgown, completely careless of the morning chill. The cold she feels does not come from outside and her shiver is from the realisation that the whole evening had been her idea.

Whatever happens now – and she has a fair idea – she is the agent. It seemed simple enough: make some new friends, get Marcus out of himself for a while, make Mary feel back at home… Yet this woman will make herself at home wherever she chooses. Tell me, what's in the lasagne, Beth? What are those flowers called, Beth?

And what's the name of these nasty little red ants that are now criss-crossing the garden path in their dozens and have made two new nests in the immaculate lawn?

IV Mercy

Uc!ram shivers with the cold and wraps the skins more tightly around himself as the dawn spills its pale silvery light across the waters and eases around the huts far below. There is a deathly quiet on the mountain as even the birds seem to be keeping their distance. In the bay he can make out their one remaining seaworthy ship tacking its way home with the light breeze, no doubt empty of any catch. A few thin, barren animals huddle together at the foot of the opposite hillside, but otherwise not a living soul can be seen. He had thought to appeal to the gods by his own suffering up here, by laying himself bare in humility before the altar and confessing his confusion of mind and weakness of spirit. Perhaps he would be granted a dream of revelation. But the gods are not interested in an individual's suffering and, in any case, you can't dream if you can't sleep.

Instead, throughout the night his disbelieving mind has been plagued by visions as, so it seemed, season upon season overtook the village cowering helplessly below at the mercy of some mad devil. A frenzied, accelerating procession of storm, flood, calm, growth, attack… lifetimes seemed to pass before him completely beyond control or reason.

Uc!ram stands up, stretches his aching body and shrugs. Well, either someone is playing a game with them or he has simply lost his mind. Anyway, there is nothing whatever he can do about it so it's time to give up.

And in this very moment, a slight movement within the sacred grove beyond the altar catches his eye. Instinctively fearing an attack, he crouches down and takes hold of a rock, the bloodied one he used on himself last night, but immediately realises his own foolishness. There has never been, there could never be, any act of violence in this holiest of places. And if despite that all the rules have indeed changed, all tradition broken, and Mount Tai – the very place where Heaven and Earth meet – were to be desecrated… Well then, there would indeed be no point in living. So he stands up, dropping the rock and the skins to face the intruder naked, unashamed and defiant.

He is more than a little taken aback to see the girl smiling back at him with evident amusement. She is somehow ageless, pale and slender, with pure white hair that falls straight to her waist and she wears a thin black robe that caresses her body as she steps forward. The old man is entranced by her serene smile and strange eyes, then realises with a shock that she is blind.

"You called me," she says simply.

"I did?"

"Yes, during the dark night."

"But who—"

"Marisa. I am a healer."

"Ah. And can you heal this?"

He sweeps out an arm across the scene below. The village is awakening and he can see figures moving like little stickmen across the open ground, hear faint cries of greeting. Strangely, even a laugh. And there seems to be much excited activity at the quayside. The sun is up now, warmly bathing the earth as the last shadows of night race for cover beneath the trees on the green hillside.

Something is different. The priest frowns.

"No, that is for you to do," she answers. "No-one else can do it. I am only here for you. You called me."

Uc!ram has spent virtually the entire night calling out, in one way or another, to all the gods his tribe has ever known. He wasn't sure what to expect, but it certainly wasn't a beautiful young... what is she, a nymph?

"Where do you come from?"

"Beyond the mountain," she says simply, waving an arm vaguely behind her.

"There is nothing beyond the mountain."

"Then I am nothing."

She has continued to approach him, inexorably slowly yet with sure feet that avoid every stone and hollow until at last she stands next to him now, very close, very gentle, and clearly seeing right through him. An energy he has not felt before begins to flood through him and wash him clean. He begins to tremble and to melt, and for a moment he still fights against it.

"No, spirit, whatever you are. This madness cannot be healed. I didn't call you."

But it is beyond words already. He has tried with heart and mind to keep the faith. But everything he has believed in has failed. All the rules have changed. He has been emptied.

V Black Monday

Marcus stares challengingly at the screen where the figures jump and chatter in their regular little square boxes as normal. Twenty years of instinct are telling him that something is going down somewhere, yet the markets are steadfastly keeping a straight face. It's just a normal day. He's closed five deals and it's barely lunchtime. The cool, airy office around him is calmly going about its business with Japan and Paris, New York and Bonn and a clutch of other screens smiling serenely back at their relaxed, wealthy minders.

So why is Marcus intensely winding a pencil between his fingers, and why can he feel sweat at the back of his neck? Well, yes, he's been strangely out of sorts since Friday evening, feeling edgy and getting irritable with Beth, not sleeping well. He has been annoyed that a Chinese schoolgirl still seems to have the better of him (he's clicked on the mountain icon but nothing appeared to change) and that a young, slim doctor with small, perfect breasts kept... His mobile 'phone moves in the shirt pocket above his heart.

"Hi, it's Mary."

Something has changed.

"How did you get my number? I'm at work."

"I should hope so. Someone has to keep the economy going. And I asked Beth for it."

"Beth knew you'd call me?" He finds himself almost whispering, glancing around himself as though to check whether others can hear. But then, why should he care?

"Of course. Honesty is the first rule, don't you think? You don't sound very pleased to hear me."

"Sorry, I'm a bit out of sorts, that's all. Yes, well... um, how are you?"

"Hungry. I'm heading for the Thai restaurant on Bank Street. Know it? Left out of your office and second right. See you in ten minutes."

And she's gone. Marcus looks at the screen again and shrugs, since the decision has been taken out of his hands. He stands up and reaches for his jacket, noticing from the corner of an eye Solomon shooting him a sickly, knowing grin.

"I looked up the I Ching," she says once they've sat down with their drinks, a claret and a mineral water. "Oh, it's an ancient Chinese book. Shih is the seventh chapter and it means an army, although not necessarily a fighting force. I mean, it's symbolic – the power stored up within a group of people under a strong and benevolent leader. And T'ai is a state of perfect harmony between the people and their environment. That's chapter eleven.

"So if you put those two together you have enormous energy, the people led by the right man and committed to their work, gathering all the resources they need, staying safe and – the most important bit – in balance with their world. That's the point of the game, do you see?"

Marcus is hardly listening to a word but he can see. What he sees, despite the hair pulled back rather sternly today and the casual denims, is a beautiful, vivacious young woman with a happy smile and dark eyes that are looking back right through him. She is continuing with something about Andy saying that the numbers seven and eleven put together in the right way are very strange in Maths and give you a result that has no fixed value, something irrational.

This at least he can believe. Whatever is happening here and now certainly isn't reasonable.

"Listen," she goes on determinedly, putting a hand on his. He jumps slightly with the surge of energy through his body. "I'm sure it's no accident that you've come across this silly game, as you call it, or that it's causing you such stress. It's not a random thing. Life tells us things we need to know if we're willing to listen. We think we know how it all works but then it keeps changing, there's always something out of control, something… wild, see? So there's something you need to change. By the way, what is it exactly that you do?"

He pauses, looks at her hand and then her eyes, and decides to trust her. And for the first time since Friday afternoon he smiles.

"I'm a futures dealer."

Her laugh shatters the calm of the entire restaurant and he joins in. God, what a relief.

Over lunch he manages to get her to talk a little about her work abroad, the continuous militia conflicts displacing thousands of people despite independence, and the basic medicine she practised. She herself had been arrested by the Indonesians but she wouldn't talk about that, or about how she'd got away. She does insist, however, as their meal ends, that he walk across London Bridge with her to Guy's and see what she is doing now.

"Well, I'm not sure," he hesitates, "I ought to get back." But another rule snaps as the 'phone moves again in his pocket.

"Are you so important that they can't manage without you for an hour?" she teases. "Or are you not rich enough? The future will still be there when you get back, you know." That, at least, is unarguable. He turns the 'phone off.

Visiting the genetics research laboratory is a humbling experience. It isn't just that some of the jumble of equipment they edge carefully past is highly lethal or even that there's more high technology per square foot than his own office. It's the distinct feeling of self-consciousness, business suit beneath lab coat, talking to these young people

47

in their jeans and tee-shirts who work longer hours than him, are better educated and who probably earn even less than Andrew. Moreover, all these resources, both hard and soft, are massed in attack against disease. At the moment it's leukaemia.

They sit drinking weak coffee from paper cups in the entrance foyer later, Marcus mesmerised by the seemingly interminable turning of the huge glass doors as a constant stream of patients come and go. Perhaps a few are even getting better.

"But even when we know every detail of the human genome," Mary is saying, "we won't stop disease. There will always be other factors, things we can't control. There will be new diseases, virus mutations and the like."

"That's a depressing thought," Marcus sympathises, missing the point.

"No, it's not at all, Marcus." She stands up, now frustrated that this strong, intelligent man seems to be so alienated from the reality of life. "This is what it means to be human. The mystery... the beauty of it all, and the challenge. It's why we have to go on caring – and never stop trying.

"If you don't respect nature then all the power in the world is worthless. Can't you see? Shih-T'ai is about power and how you use it. What do you use yours for, Marcus? Oh, for heaven's sake," it becomes too much for her, "go and roll your dice."

She has disappeared back through the crowd before he can open his mouth. Not that he has the faintest idea what to say. In fact, Marcus barely speaks another word for the rest of the day.

Feeling somehow like a guilty schoolboy not sure of which rule he's broken this time, he wanders back across the Thames to find that all hell has broken out in the office. There is paper strewn everywhere and more than one monitor lies smashed on the floor. Solomon is sitting nearby with his head in his hands. Others who were friends a couple of hours ago now glare malevolently at him as he enters.

revealed a clear vision that she recognises, with little surprise, as having been waiting there for years.

It's her husband's birthday tomorrow so she walks down to the corner shop to buy fruit, a box of chocolates, a card and a women's magazine, keeping up a cheerful conversation with the shopkeeper for the sake of it. Is she planning a night out, maybe even a holiday, a special treat? Something like that. When she gets home she has coffee and starts on the chocolates before settling down at his computer; then she takes out the cheap 'phone she bought yesterday and makes a few calls. Satisfied that everything is in place, she goes up to the loft to retrieve a large suitcase and an overnight bag before printing off two documents and erasing the search history.

By the evening Marcus has recovered some of his spirit and is even talking about setting up on his own. It hasn't been a total disaster. After all, wars happen all the time. You take your losses and move on. In any case, most of their money is in offshore accounts; it will just take a bit of time to release what they need. Beth smiles indulgently when he says he just needs a bit of time in his study before turning in.

Next morning she brings him breakfast in bed and the birthday card, kisses him fondly and tells him that she loves him. And then, as he's leaving for the station 'to clear things up and see some people', she smiles and says there'll be a nice surprise for him later. Thank heavens, he thinks to himself, everything is normal, and he pauses at the corner to turn and wave.

She gives it twenty-five minutes then calls in sick and stands motion-less in the garden for a good while, hearing the silence – not even a bird – and saying a prayer to whichever gods might happen to be listening. Back inside, she visits each room in turn briefly, lingering a moment in his study. The computer screen is saying, "Congratulations! You have reached Level Seven. Are you ready for the final challenge?" and despite everything she is still laughing to herself as she closes the front door.

Marcus spends much of the morning in nose to nose negotiation with Solomon until, allowing himself a deep breath of satisfaction, he decides he has got most of what he had hoped for out of the day. Back at his own desk, though, he is somewhat taken aback to find his own overnight bag sitting there. No, no-one knows, it has been delivered by a courier. Inside, there is a change of clothes and a wash-bag. There's an envelope on the desk, too, containing two notices on headed paper. One is from the Royal Albert Hall saying that his ticket for this evening's performance of Four Last Songs by Richard Strauss can be collected at the Box Office. The other confirms his reservation for tonight at a small Kensington hotel.

This is a fun game. If truth be told, Marcus shut the door on child-hood long ago and turned to the simple pursuit of financial security and the comforts it brings. But now he feels something melt within and dabs at the corner of one eye as his world lightens. Beth is a remarkable woman.

He has a leisurely lunch at the Thai restaurant where somehow Mary's energy seems to linger. They did not part well the other day yet her last words still swirl in his mind from time to time. The game is about power and how you use it. Well, one game is coming to an end and there are moves to be planned for the future. After lunch he takes in an exhibition at the Tate, pausing every so often to make notes in his pocket book, before checking into the hotel, making a few calls and having a rest.

Music has never been a great part of his life, a passing acquain-tance rather than a friend, but in the evening he sits back and lets it wash through him, his eyes closed. It is just a little worrying that the seat next to his has remained empty – something must have come up at school or the traffic was really bad – yet at this moment it doesn't matter anymore that he has no idea what's going on. For the first time in perhaps many years, he begins to let go and allow things to happen.

Towards the end of Im Abendrot, the soprano intones "Ist dies etwa der Tod?" and the seven-note phrase of the transfiguration theme takes hold of one's spirit and leads it towards a new world.

"Your wife has arrived." The hotel receptionist turns on a plastic smile as he nods towards Marcus. "She's in your room."

There is champagne cooling on a small table alongside fresh flowers and Belgian chocolates, and the sound of running water from the bathroom. Marcus suddenly, unaccountably, feels a nervous sweat on his neck and loosens his tie. Again, something doesn't feel right. For the last week his mind has been pulled inside out. He hasn't seen it. Beside him, his wife has been supportive and loving. He hasn't seen her. There have been hidden, unresolved conflicts just beneath the surface of his world and they've been spreading for years. He hasn't seen them.

All along, there has been a plan, a child's game with rules far too simple to understand. Now he sees it. Because the next thing he sees is Mary, emerging from the shower as beautiful as he has imagined her. She smiles and picks up a bath robe, then drops it and walks slowly towards him.

VII   End game

Ad!yn is changed. They all are, of course, with these strange new seasons, but it is in him that the transformation is the most remarkable. The anger has gone, along with the bitterness over his bereavement, and in place of a young man's blind and disrespectful rebelliousness is a calm vision and a maturity beyond his years. It is not that he has somehow softened. Rather, if anything, his strength and determination have simply developed to a point where they can be recognised in a single word or gesture.

When Uc!ram comes down from the mountain on that eerily quiet morning, now etched in the folklore of the village, everyone can see that he is a different man. He doesn't have to say anything, to explain himself, to announce any gods' intentions or the judgement of any stones. You can just see it. The torture of his soul has disappeared. And whilst, by his own pronouncement, he will no longer be their priest, his authority is renewed.

Now he is their healer. From somewhere in that dark night has come a great gift. This first morning, intuitively and without any ritual, he has lain his hand on a sick child and calmed the fever away. Next, a young man's battle wound has been closed up, the pain dismissed. And so it goes on throughout the first day, as the people quietly go about putting their lives back together, mending homes and nets and turning the soil over.

In the evening, for the last time, he calls the people together around the fire to tell them how things will be. Lies!a will assume the priesthood, being of the lineage, with Ad!yn as her first minister, learning the ways. This is accepted without question. True, it is unknown in the tribe's memory for a woman to lead them. But these are new times, everyone can see that.

For the time being, living alone at the edge of the forest, Uc!ram will be on hand to guide Ad!yn in the ways of the gods on the mountain. There will be new ways of living, too, that the spirit has taught him. The animals are to be kept for their milk and their wool only, not for meat. New crops will be planted and Uc!ram knows where to find the seeds. Most surprising is that he and Ad!yn will go together and make peace with the Am!der, who have also suffered greatly in recent times, so that they can share their knowledge and work together.

"All this, the spirit taught me," he ends, "so that we may be granted seven seasons with neither flood nor plague. When they return, as is the way of nature, we shall be stronger."

The people smile to one another and talk quietly. They could not have imagined this future, in which all the rules will change, yet it feels right.

Marcus finds three messages on his 'phone from Beth, asking where he is. They must have arrived while it was switched off during the concert. Later, a solicitor calls at the Royal Albert Hall Box Office and the hotel Reception, and it is confirmed that the bookings were made by a Mary Davidson and charged to the credit card of a Marcus Boyd.

Later still, Marcus has set up a medical research foundation whilst Beth has turned his study into a studio and has pretensions of being an artist.

Memory

I watched your body arching
skin bathed
in the early sacred light of morning
when all hearts beat slower
and minds' eyes shift from side to side
in fear of death

and every hair
and every pore of you
each quiet cry
each soft and naked phrase you whispered
was reminding me
to live

"Where the fuck have you been, Marcus? And why's your fucking 'phone turned off? Having fun were we? Well, so were we, Marcus, so were we. As you can see."

"You should have been here, Marcus. You might have been able—"

"It's your job to be here and—"

"This is your place, Marcus."

"You've no idea what's going on, have you, sunshine? Well, old son, there's a fucking war on, that's all. A fucking war. And all your fucking futures are down the toilet."

VI The Gift

It takes Beth the best part of thirty-six hours to work out the whole story and get Marcus to begin talking about it, let alone assess its full impact. Life does, however, rather seem to be trying to tell them something and she is the first to hear it.

He has gone into the office as usual on Tuesday to see whether any pieces can be picked up and put back together, but has come home early and shut himself away in the study until evening. They eat the meal she has prepared and then sit together beneath the patio canopy until the early hours, looking out at the changing face of the garden beneath a clear, starlit sky. The trees cast haunting shadows across the grass, swaying gently in the breeze, as the gathering dusk swallows up each carefully placed feature. Barely a dozen sentences apiece are exchanged. She spends much of the time trying to remember the names of the various constellations, which she had been made to learn as a child, and making up new ones instead.

The next morning Marcus leaves for the City hollow-eyed and crumple-suited. It's Beth's day off from school but she knows exactly how to fill the time. That hidden inner door has opened fully and

Tonight

tonight
the wind rolls on a sea of thought
and suburban streetlights swirl
like signal lamps
on ghostly tallship masts

while you
the galley slave of my drowned dreams
pull at me
as though our very lives depended on
tonight

Figures with Moon

57

Witching Hour

moon
fuller by the minute
fills up my window
seeping into me with waves of anger
dashed upon rocks of certain knowledge
that I am not free

white moon
strung up against the blackness
teaching me
an abject lesson in
surrender

throwing stones at it
may tide me over
for another month

The Gifts Of Nature

"Oh my…" I stopped myself just in time. Expressions of genuine shock have been so devalued these days and only draw attention when it's not called for. The last thing I would have wanted was to embarrass her.

It was a cool March day with weak sunlight fringing the light clouds over London, but the air was fresh with a promise of spring. I had recently discovered this café that sold wonderful French patisseries and the best coffee I had tasted for years. Just as pleasing, up a few steps at the back was a quiet room where one could sit undisturbed, reading a book or turning things over in the mind. I had just folded my coat over the back of a chair and settled down, reaching for the spoon, when I heard a light cough. Somehow you know, don't you, when everything has changed.

A couple of tables away from me, poring over a sketchpad with pencil in mid-air, tumbling auburn hair framing a thin, drawn yet unmistakable face, was Sophie. I hadn't seen her for, what, thirty years or so but there are people you will always recognise however much life has trampled over them. Back then we had been art students, full of energy and outrageous plans that we somehow knew would never work; that didn't matter in the slightest, of course, because we had our whole lives ahead of us and there would always be other plans. She and I had been close friends for a while and we'd even worked together on a design project, a kind of game for… well, that's not relevant except that it had been great fun. In this moment, a flood of happy memories and a few regrets rushed through my mind.

Now Sophie was sitting alone with her green tea, staring down at the paper and looking old, her body thin, her skin lined and with a tinge of grey. She coughed quietly again and brought her hand to her mouth, dropping the pencil but seeming not to notice. I picked up my cappuccino and moved across, retrieved the pencil from under the table and sat down opposite her without speaking, waiting for the moment. After perhaps a minute, she looked up and smiled slowly, making a strange, small nod of her head as she recognised me.

"It's good to see you," I began, pausing because I was not at all sure how to go on. "You look, um…"

"Yes, I know," she said, her voice deeper than it had been and coming with some effort, as though from far away inside her. "It's a brain tumour. Inoperable." She always had been pretty direct. But those words froze my whole being in my seat, incapable of any movement or response.

With the two of us, passing years were as nothing because our inner selves – the soul, if you like, that is bound inextricably to other souls despite the various outer coats they are obliged to wear in this life – were unchanged by experiences that come and go. It makes you think that such people must have shared many lifetimes together. Back then in this one, we'd been a force of nature together, sharing thoughts, finishing each other's sentences and laughing at unspoken jokes. Some of our friends were surprised that we hadn't stayed together after college, when life offered us different paths. But it had never been that kind of relationship, just a closeness that never dissolves. So thinking about it all now, I suppose it was inevitable that we should meet again before it was too late.

"I'm glad it's you," she broke into my thoughts after a couple of minutes' silence. "Every meeting has a purpose, don't you think? And I had a feeling, an intuition perhaps, that there'd be a meeting today. See, there isn't much time. That's why I came here. I'm so glad it's you." She smiled wanly again, apparently satisfied that all was as it should be.

Sophie never was one for small talk. It's a valuable social skill, they say, but entirely superfluous to us. There was no exchange of news, like, 'What have you been up to for thirty years?' or 'Do you have a family?' Neither of us cared about such things right now because all that mattered was what was happening here and what we needed to share. Our personal histories, like so much else in life when it really comes down to it, were ephemeral.

Our drinks grew cold, equally forgotten. A waitress wearing the traditional French lace apron and with her long dark hair tied sternly back, silently removed them and, a few minutes later, returned with fresh ones. I would reflect later, indeed every time I visited the place, that this is what actually made it special: it was not the cakes and coffee, good as they were, but the air of simple and kind human understanding that allows people to be in their moment, without question. Others around us knew this too, absorbed in their own quiet conversations, reading books or newspapers, working at laptops, no-one remotely interested in eavesdropping. Equally there was an unspoken acceptance that one should not occupy this oasis for too long, unless it were necessary, and one by one the tables around us were vacated and refilled by others who knew the ways.

It was a precious place and time, so rare in our unnatural world, and just rather unfortunate, if entirely appropriate, that it was meant to host this particular reunion.

After some time, I have no idea how long, Sophie seemed to have resolved all the competing troubled thoughts in her mind and decided on the words that were required. Slowly, she closed the sketchpad and reached out a hand so that her fingers closed lightly over mine. As she looked across at me, her face visibly brightened a little.

"You mustn't feel pity," she began, her voice barely audible yet cutting deeply within me. "There's no point in that. Some sadness is inevitable, I suppose, because after all this time... and we were such good friends... you probably hoped that—" her fingers waved the air dismissively "—but pity isn't appropriate. It's just nature. It's being human, it's how it is.

"Countless people suffer far more than I have, die much younger, even small children. Or they go through their entire lives disfigured or sick. It's just... life. I mean, when you walked along the pavement to get here surrounded by people all going about their normal business... or when you traipse around the supermarket with everyone going up and down the aisles choosing their beans and cheese... do you have any idea how many of them are struggling with invisible illnesses or disabilities? One in five people have arthritis and one in four will have a mental illness someday. Children are born with cerebral palsy, autism, Downs and one in fifteen... sorry!" She shrugged as she sat back and there was that small, enigmatic smile again. "I've been working for a charity."

"I do get your point," I conceded, mentally filing away the information to research properly later. "All the same, you're not a statistic. Not to me. And I'm having trouble understanding how you seem to be so philosophical about this thing that's happened to you. This... irrational, cruel thing that's ruined all your hopes and dreams of what you wanted to do and achieve in your life."

"No, not at all. You haven't got it, have you?" Suddenly, she was more animated, sitting up straight and taking a long drink of her tea. She looked over my shoulder and out across the café, through its wide window to the tree-lined street and the heathland beyond, drinking that in too. "Life is beautiful. And my life has been wonderful, even if it has been painful at times and shorter than I might have expected. There's nothing philosophical about it. It's reality. This is how it is being human. There's no reasoning with it. You can't make value judgements about it."

My head was a whirlpool of thoughts and feelings, trying to get a handle on this outlier of suddenly meeting a dear friend yet within minutes being thrust into a personal argument about... what, existentialism? Then there was a brief flash of clarity in my mind as I spotted a flaw in it all.

"But look," I began, stirring the sugar into my fresh coffee and ruining the carefully sprinkled chocolate heart design on the froth, "earlier on you said that everything has a purpose. Now you're suggesting that all these illnesses and disabilities – and this awful thing that's happened to you – are just accidents of nature. Well you can't have it both ways."

"Ah, so you have got it after all," she almost laughed. The young Sophie re-emerged in her eyes for a moment and the lines of her face softened a little. "That's exactly what they are. Accidents. Like falling off a horse and losing the use of your legs. Things happen, and it's the price we pay for the wonder of being human. But there's no *higher* purpose to it.

"Oh, I know some people like to believe that we all make a so-called soul contract before we're born and agree to have our lives mangled up for some perverse spiritual reason. It's karma, they say. But that's just looking for excuses. A desperate attempt to make sense of something that just isn't, like you said, rational. It's a need for some kind of control where there isn't any. Perhaps I used to think like that once, too."

Her head leaned to one side and her eyes lost their focus as though she were reviewing her life and re-evaluating every thought. For myself,

I also couldn't help instantly being taken back to some particular decisions I'd made over the years in an effort to make life turn the way I thought I wanted it to, rather than allowing it to flow, to find its natural course. You only have to look up at the sky on a clear night to realise how very insignificant we are, how powerless. And then when partners or colleagues just don't behave as we hope or expect them to, is it not reasonable to want to get back some kind of control?

"But when you work with the disabled," her quiet words cut into my thoughts before they could turn to regret, "you see that it's simply nature.

"On the other hand," she leaned forward now and made an odd circling motion in the air between us with her teaspoon as if to bring our talk back to its beginning, "the human mind, here and now, has the most incredible ability to know things and somehow connect with other people's minds. It doesn't have to be a spiritual thing – it's probably just biochemistry we don't understand yet, a sixth sense, or a seventh. So no, there's no purpose in my tumour but, yes, there's definitely a purpose in our meeting here today."

We sat in silence for several minutes then as I tried to digest this flood. It was more to think about than I'd had for months, yet something told me at the same time that there was little point in thought. It was a matter of feeling and of acceptance. The drinks went cold again. Eventually, Sophie raised herself unsteadily to her feet, gathered up her sketchpad and light raincoat, and looked me coolly in the face. All I could do was raise an eyebrow. She asked me to meet her in two weeks' time, at the special place we used to go to in the park together, when we were full of energy with our whole lives ahead of us.

"I'll have a gift for you," she said. "Don't worry, it's a good one."

It was a quiet day just before Easter. On reflection, this was entirely appropriate. The cold and darkness of winter had receded further now, the trees were coming into leaf and some early wild flowers were appearing hesitantly in the hedgerows as though testing the air. Light clouds flowed lazily across the sky and this area of the park was at peace, still too chilly for many people. All the same, there was a tension in the air, that sense of a turning point being reached. But that was probably just me.

I saw Sophie coming from some fifty yards away and even at that distance I could see her smile and a strangely lighter aura around her despite her rather laboured steps. My heart jumped a little, ridiculously, just as it had done all those years ago but now was just too late and inappropriate. She was carrying a holdall that she set down beside me as she caught her breath, and from which she then took a blanket for the dewy ground. Neither of us had spoken. With a small theatrical flourish she then took out two flasks, one of green tea for her and the other with coffee for me, and a white, thin card box which she opened to reveal fresh cream cakes from the French café. She had always been thoughtful. I suppose the cakes were meant to soften the impact, this perhaps being the last time we would see one another. She knelt down and poured the drinks for us.

"I shall be leaving very soon," she said at last, as direct as ever. "The doctors say it could be months, maybe six, maybe nine. You know what they're like. For all their brilliant minds and years of training they're useless at telling you how it really is. Anyway, I'm not going to wait for that. Wasting away and becoming helpless isn't my style." That was true enough. "When you know how it really is, when the path you're on is ending and there aren't any other paths, there's no point walking is there?"

"Unless," I ventured, through tears that wouldn't be held back, "there's some hidden new path you don't know about yet?" It was as though the very nature around us paused in its growth now and became still, watching us and hanging on our words. "What about, I don't know, what do they call it – alternative therapy?"

"Been there, done that. There's a reason it's called 'alternative' – it doesn't work. Anyway, not for me. I know where I'm going."

"A spirit world? Is that what you believe in?" That was clumsy, I know, but normal thoughts were failing me.

"You mean passing over? Or just passing. No-one knows, not for sure. I prefer just to say that I'm leaving and I have no idea where the adventure of life will take me next. No, look," she held up a hand as I opened my mouth to object again, then placed her fingers lightly onto mine as she had done in the café, "I'm not being brave or anything like that. Please try to accept it. This is just how it is."

I did come to accept it, though it took a considerable time as leaving always does, and maybe that in itself would have been enough of a gift. In these brief final minutes shared together, Sophie taught me that sometimes we have to stop thinking, stop trying to make sense of things.

We ate our cakes and sat in silence for goodness knows how long, as close as we had ever been, until at last she got painfully to her feet and packed away the things. Before leaving, however, she reached into a side pocket of the holdall and brought out a small, brown paper bag. I had completely forgotten about this, the reason for our meeting.

"I know you still think there's something cruel about all this, about life," she said, gesturing to me to get up beside her. "But nature doesn't do ethics. And she has a lot more to think about, to care about, than human beings. Still, she does offer us many gifts and this is one of them."

To my astonishment, she then took from the paper bag a small bunch of what looked like grapes. There were seven of them, dark purple and firm. She carefully broke off three of them and put them in the pocket of her jacket before handing the others to me in the paper bag, laughing aloud at the bemused expression on my face.

"Three or four of these will help you to leave peacefully with no fuss when the time comes. With no pain. But only when you're ready, of course. Just keep them in a cool place. I'm sure that three will be enough for me so the others are my gift to you. You're bigger than me. Let's say it's in memory of all the wonderful times we had. And maybe could have had."

I was utterly incapable of speaking as I looked down incredulously at the innocuous paper bag, and when I looked up again Sophie was already at the edge of the park, turning to give me one final wave. A rush of pain and regret flooded through me as I realised there hadn't been a last embrace, even a few words from me of… comfort? Gratitude? I knew she wouldn't have minded but I still felt foolish.

A week later, I received a letter from her together with a note from her mother saying that Sophie had passed away quietly in her sleep, painlessly and with all the lines of her face smoothed away. The letter was a pretty accurate recollection of our conversations in the French café and there in the park. There was nothing wrong with her mind, then. Which is just as well…

Everything that I have described happened about twenty years ago and, thanks to that last letter, I remember it all as if it were yesterday. The trouble is, though, I can't actually remember what did happen yesterday. It's not just going into a room and forgetting what I went in for, which everybody does from time to time. No, I don't remember which football team I've supported all my life. When the post arrives

I don't know who it's for, and I don't remember my daughter's name when she visits. I couldn't tell you whether I like pasta or what I really enjoyed watching on TV last week. My old spinal injury has had its way with me too, so I can't walk much and my bedroom's been moved downstairs.

I do have a carer who comes in every day, but I couldn't tell you her name though she seems very kind. I got her to buy me a small voice recorder so I could dictate all this because I don't recognise all the letters on the computer keyboard anymore and she said she'll get someone to type it up. That was kind of her. Because somehow it feels important for the story to be told, partly in memory of my dear friend, of course, but also because of what she taught me about being human... how we cannot judge nature. Yet we can live our lives to the full and care about others. This was an act, you could say, at the edge of love.

I think it will soon be time to use Sophie's gift for myself. Like her, wasting away and becoming helpless isn't my style. I had put the paper bag away in a cupboard untouched because I had no idea what to think about it. Then recently I took it out expecting the fruit to be rotten and I'd have to throw them away anyway. But they're still perfectly firm and ripe.

So I shall use them. For once, I can be in control. And I think it's good to know that whatever life's... challenges... accidents... the weaknesses of the body... and even when the path we're on is ending... nature has gifts for us.

Out of Body, Out of Mind

Ellie gently pushed the bedroom door and moved in silently on bare feet, feeling a happy warmth flow around and within her like a calm wave on a summer evening beach. It crept and edged its way to every part, relaxing the muscles of her eyes, easing down her shoulders and dissolving that small habitual tension at the side of her mouth. Just seeing Neil's head asleep on her pillow, one arm limp over the side of the bed, and hearing his quiet, shallow breath was enough. She hadn't believed this feeling possible.

A trace of lavender hung in the air from the oil burner as she slipped out of her clothes by the flickering last light of the candle. The day's events ran through her mind. Every few seconds, though, she stopped the thoughts and made herself rewind to get each moment in perfect sequence and to savour it again.

They had so few days together like this and today had been special. They had driven into the unfamiliar New Forest countryside and meandered through quiet lanes and villages with windows open to the clean air. They had exchanged smiles with local people going about their own normal weekend lives, oblivious to how far from normal was this couple's day. They'd been safe, where nobody knew them. In the city there was the danger at every turn that someone might recognise one of them, rock the boat and ruin this new life growing delicately between them like a crystal. This taste of freedom, after so many evenings indoors behind closed curtains, had been sweet.

At lunchtime they had found an old pub in the middle of nowhere, the bar busy with farmers in work clothes mixing easily and noisily with other townspeople like themselves, escaping their stresses. The food was simple, the conversation light – there had never been an awkward silence between them for a moment – and, when she had casually remarked over coffee that all she needed to complete the meal was a mint wafer, he had slipped away on some pretext and returned with a whole box from the nearby local shop. Ellie had to put her hand over her mouth to stop herself giggling aloud with pleasure at the memory.

Neil hated shopping and wasting time with equal intensity, but to please her they had driven further and played with foolish smiles at being tourists in Burley, visiting the small shops and buying completely unnecessary gifts for friends and their children. She had lingered like a child herself in front of the china teddy bears, a tear squeezing from one eye as they touched that buried nerve and took her back instantly to a moment of safety amid the dark shadows of her childhood. And when they finally got home in the early evening and he had pressed the small figure into her hand – he must have bought it when he pretended to slip back to the car for the camera – a final door had been unlocked and she had fallen into his arms.

Slowly coming back to the moment, Ellie caught sight of herself in the long wall mirror. Her body was soft in the candlelight yet strong and confident, and her consciousness felt fully centred within her for perhaps the first time. She had been waiting for such a feeling all her life, to be whole.

But none of these thoughts would be of any help at all in twelve hours' time. Absolutely nothing could have prepared her for what was to happen.

She blew out the candle and slipped into bed hoping not to wake him, but his body turned instinctively towards her and they folded around one another, breath on breath, melting. Perhaps somewhere deep in his subconscious he would sense her feelings. And far within her own mind, the touch triggered some distant secret lever she had never suspected was there and she began to feel something else. The earlier warmth had continued to grow as it filled her yet its calm wave had not after all reached its peak and turned to ebb. It continued to flow on and build and rise up until now it overcame her in a tidal flood that submerged every thought she had so carefully nurtured of this day.

Ellie caught her breath, at first fighting the loss of control, until it came through with a sob and a rush of tears despite herself. She found herself now on an entirely different level, rising above herself. Yes, she had known love before, its passion and caring, and no matter that it had always ended as all things do, no matter that she had never quite been able to make it last – some fault in her emotional design, perhaps – for she had still known more good times than many do. Yet now… she was touching something beyond imagination. She realised that for the first time she truly loved another person more than herself. At this point it was as though her spirit eased itself free of her, to drift up over the bed and sense its oneness with all that is.

"What is it?" Neil murmured, still more than half asleep. But her reply could not be heard. In any case, there are no words to describe what is beyond comprehension.

Ellie was up first on Sunday morning. She hadn't slept much but that didn't matter as the feelings of the previous day had stayed with her while she lay back calmly, one arm across him, watching the thin shafts of light from passing cars filter through a chink in the curtains and trace their patterns above her head, picking out the ceiling relief. Her body was alive with this new and subtle energy and she neither needed rest nor wanted to be unconscious. No-one should sleep through the best moments of their lives.

Most of the night she had just bathed in the whole experience, although every so often the left brain had intruded for a few moments to wonder what all this would mean for them, for their future. Surely now, after all the uncertainty… She had loved him from the first moment they'd met by chance at the health club two years before – at least, she had sensed that they belonged together – when she wandered into the wrong class and stood there, embarrassed, as their eyes met. She hadn't been surprised when he called her a couple of days later to invite her to join the class anyway, and her confession that she hadn't done any serious exercise for years brought only a delighted laugh and an invitation for dinner.

They were a couple before the coffee arrived. And before he told her that he was married. It didn't matter.

As time passed, the pleasure of being with him – it was always on Thursday evenings with the very occasional 'weekend conference' – had never dimmed once. Of course, she had cried herself to sleep at times when she imagined him playing with his children or being alone with his wife (he said they were estranged and never slept together, yet...), but she was learning patience and forbearance, which were wonderful discoveries. She knew she could wait because the two of them were inevitable.

Yes, she had faltered once when after a year there was no sign of him taking action and a straightforward friend had told her that she was being used. Carl had been attractive, clever and single, and she had seduced herself into the briefest of affairs. And despite the whole world's opinion on these things, she had felt ashamed of betraying her married lover. She had confessed and begged forgiveness and learned all over again how to wait. If anything, their love had even seemed to her to grow deeper after that as she realised with great clarity that this kind and gentle man was simply fearful – of the pain he knew he would have to cause and of the loss of family life he had longed for after his own difficult childhood.

Still, it had to be. The marriage didn't work and the children were being hurt anyway. She had supported him at every step, listening to his anxieties, holding him when he became quiet, knowing that she would receive her reward. Now, this Sunday morning, the future was clear and everything was coming together.

One more memory of the previous day came to mind and almost made her laugh aloud. After a simple dinner they had sat close together on her sofa to watch some pointless television show and then a film she had wanted to see for ages came on. It was a tragic love story and she was just in the mood for it, completely relaxed beneath his arm. Neil had said he was tired by all the fresh air, walking and driving and wanted to sleep so had gone upstairs while she stayed in the story. It was the first time they had shared a night and not gone to bed at the same time. Just as though they were already married.

Beaming like a child, Ellie slipped out of bed leaving him to sleep on, taking her clothes downstairs to dress before quietly letting herself out of the front door into the bright early sunlight of a spring day. The third of May. She almost skipped the few hundred yards to the local shops, returning with his favourite bagels and cream cheese from the delicatessen and a heavy newspaper with its many travel, film and sports supplements. Breakfast tray prepared, she took a shower, the cascading water massaging every pore until she felt cleaner than she had ever been. With her back pressed against the glass screen, she heard him enter the bathroom and the anticipation shook her whole body. He slid back the glass, kissed the back of her neck and caressed her breasts… then turned round and went out.

World's End

Neil didn't know what to say, his discomfort so palpable and his fear of showing it so great that he simply kept quiet. The breakfast was good and Ellie was purring like a kitten, her feelings overflowing around them both so powerfully that his own were submerged. He had never seen her so happy. Unequal to the struggle, he did as so many men have done and retreated into virtual silence.

Yet moments of revolution cannot be denied. When you find yourself on that beach and the calm summer evening has given way to a tumultuous storm and a crashing wave is about to engulf you, followed by others, you can only stand firm for a few pointlessly proud moments. A man gives himself away too easily at such times. He lingered too long over the coffee, showed too much interest in the magazine feature about an attractive businesswoman he knew slightly, showed too little interest in the sports pages. His eyes weren't focusing anyway. So finally he gave her a light kiss on the forehead and jumped out of bed to get dressed.

"I, um… I need to get going."

She sat up, bemused. There were hours of this perfect day left and he'd said they could spend the whole weekend together.

"But I thought—"

"No, I promised the boys I'd take them out. I should spend more time with them." He was still turned away from her and the words were carefully chosen not to be argued with.

"I see." Patience, she reminded herself. All the same, she pushed back the duvet and approached him with a reassuring touch, but he was already pulling his shirt on and moving away to the bathroom.

Ellie wrapped her black silk dressing gown around herself and went downstairs to make fresh coffee and wait. There was nothing else she could do. It was coming. And though every fibre of her being fought against it, refusing to realise it, and threw up a protective mist of happy memories around her, it was still coming. A tiny insignificant speck of darkness in the far distance of her mind was growing closer now and approaching with the speed of light departing. Something gripped and pulled at her stomach.

At last he came downstairs, overnight bag in one hand, magazine in the other, already on his way.

"Talk to me. Please."

He sat uncomfortably on the opposite side of the table he'd bought her, eyes downcast, the coffee cooling between them. He hesitated for a full two minutes. What the hell. People were going to get hurt anyway.

"I think... perhaps we shouldn't see each other anymore. It's been on my mind for quite a while. Everything's too much... you know, at the moment... too much stress. I need... space." There was some more, just as disjointed and limp, but Ellie didn't hear it.

"Neil—" was this voice hers? "—I've never been so happy in my life, with you. Yesterday was... and I thought—"

"I know, Ellie." For the first time he lifted his eyes to hers. He didn't fully understand how he could do this, why he had to do this, but was now sure that he had to. It was coming even faster. "I'm very fond of you..."

It was here. It was upon her. With a silent scream the bolt thudded into her forehead, shattering her mind. Did he say that? 'Fond of you'? Did he say that? Dimly, she realised that he was still talking, in a voice that was weak and excusing itself, and whilst she didn't want to hear it she forced herself back to listening because she needed every word of it, at whatever cost.

"...so it's not going to work, is it? We're too different, we don't like the same things. I mean, in everyday life. It's not going to work, is it?" She was too incredulous to answer. Of course they were different, of course they didn't share the same interests, of course she knew all that. That's exactly why their relationship was so magical, because it did work despite all the differences. It came round again for another hit.

"Look, Ellie, you're wonderful in lots of ways... you're beautiful, you're caring and patient... but sometimes I think you just don't live in the real world. Everything's in your head. It's all feelings and impulses and you don't actually see what's in front of your eyes, what's going on around you. I mean, you're always losing things, even your keys. You pick things up and put them down somewhere else then can't find them. You scratch your car and have no idea how it happened. I buy you flowers but you forget to water them so they die and you don't seem to mind. You don't notice. You don't even notice people sometimes. Yes, everyone says how friendly you are, and it's true, you'll talk to anyone. But yesterday that old guy in the shop was talking to you and you just turned away to chat to someone else. He was hurt, I saw it. You hurt people because you're inside your own head all the time. You hurt me too sometimes, Ellie."

Crushed small and barely breathing, she had to respond. This was too far. Anything in the world but that.

"I couldn't hurt you, Neil, I—"

"Ellie, you don't notice. I mean, how could you want to watch that film last night when I said I hated it and was too tired anyway? Do you realise that was the first time we haven't gone to bed together? I needed you then, I was feeling weak…" His head fell into his hands as a despairing sigh escaped his lips. "I needed you for once, but it's always about what you want. You live in your own private world."

"I'm sorry. I thought… I mean, I didn't think." She reached out a hand across the table towards his. "But I love you and I want to show you—"

He stood up abruptly, standing above her and almost shaking with anger as the next wave caught him too, shocking her back into her chair with a new kind of fear.

"Show me? When did you ever show me? Carl, was that showing me? You don't know the meaning of love. I give you gifts, I write you loving letters – you've got a drawer full of them – and when did you ever write me a letter? Any letter? Do you show an interest in my work, do you even know what I really do, what matters to me?

77

Those things are showing love. Do you realise that I've risked my marriage for you?"

Ah, so that's it. Risk. He knew he'd said too much but there was no holding it back and anyway it was too late now. The last slivers of mind disintegrated. When at last Ellie looked up he had gone. And all the space he said he needed was now inside her.

Φ

Wednesday the sixth of May. Ellie found herself still alive but had no idea whatever how she had passed the last three days. Sunday's breakfast tray still sat on the kitchen table, crumbs hardened and fruit blackening. Upstairs, bedclothes lay in a heap beside unopened newspaper supplements. She must have slept but in her clothes and probably not on the bed. Now she wandered around the house, stumbling, clutching a pillow to her face with the scent of his body on it, refusing to believe that it was already fading.

Much of the time, of course, she cried. Every so often, indeed, she wept uncontrollably for an hour or more, her body shaken by those huge waves that carried her up to their peak and spat out great howls as they fell away. And as they retreated from that scarred beach, the debris they left behind was a deep and piercing pain that started in her solar plexus and crept out along tentacles of fire to every part of her body. Then just as she thought she'd got control of it back again there was another wave, and another even greater, as the storm circled incessantly around her. Each powerful gust of wind drew in one stray memory after another... the candle-lit massage last New Year, the French wine bar with the waiter's knowing smile, their first nervous night together at that Hertfordshire inn miles from home, cooking their meal on Thursdays and waiting excitedly for the sound of his car outside… Always Thursdays, the heart of their deception.

Thursday the seventh. He wouldn't be coming. She cooked anyway and left it all uneaten. Every time a car slowed down outside she went to the window. When the 'phone rang she snatched at it and then left it on a chair unanswered. He didn't come.

So what was it that he really needed? Yes, Ellie knew now so she would have to show him, doing two things she had never done before. She wrote him a letter and filled it with every trace of reassurance her splintered mind could muster – as much time as he needed, as much space, even as many other women as he wanted, she would still be there for him. She handed it in at the health club and then went to the staff car park and tied a rose to his windscreen wipers. It was a release. But he didn't call. He didn't write.

When she hadn't turned up for work someone called and took her mumbled, incoherent reply to be illness. They didn't call again either. By the weekend she began to function a little better, clearing up, wiping surfaces, putting photographs away, washing a shirt he'd left behind before suddenly regretting that she'd touched it at all, another scent lost. But far from diminishing, the pain seemed to get worse each day as her emptiness continued to expand. The one comfort to her in all of this was the complete conviction – if she hadn't already known it – that she loved Neil with a wholeness that she'd longed for all her life. This was true. So even he could not go on denying it.

She felt not the slightest trace of anger towards him for bringing this horror into their lives because she knew it couldn't be helped, and sooner or later he would find the way for them to be at peace. Her only problem was how to survive until then. In this she found herself entirely alone. What he'd said about her getting on well with others was true and she'd had several friends. Perhaps it was also true, however, that she didn't focus well enough on them and there had been very

79

few with whom she could share anything in depth. In any case, she'd let them go these last two years. Neil being her whole life, she hadn't needed anyone else. And others had found it hard to keep any social life with someone whose lover was married.

There are times when everyone needs their mother, the warmth of blood, whatever the past. It was a mistake.

"Well, there's men for you. You wouldn't be told, would you? Never were. You'll have to sort it out for yourself, girl. Do you think you're the only one who's ever been let down by a man? Anyway, what do you think you're doing, upsetting me at my age?" There was more in the same vein, each bit laced with salt. She returned home more wounded than before, more alone, but at least she knew where she stood.

Wednesday the thirteenth of May. The abysmal ache still gripped and the tears still flowed, but Ellie's mind was clearing just enough for her to be able to reflect. The first thing she reflected on was that surely there's a limit to how many tears one person could cry in their lifetime. Then she reflected on the extraordinary devastation of her life. This was hardly the first pain she had known. There had been the loss of her wonderful, kind father, taken suddenly by illness without warning. There had been her own divorce. Yes, they married far too young but there had still been some happiness and years of trying, only to be broken up in recrimination and by infidelity and lawyers. The irony of her own part in Neil's marriage did not escape her.

But none of these things had in the least prepared her for today and its alien grief and terror. She reflected that as a child she had longed to be grown up, assuming that life must be so much easier when one is capable and free to make choices, with school and exams in the past. People never tell you that it actually gets harder, that you're never free, that you have to go on learning and each test is greater than the last. Her experiences had made her stronger, that was true. Strong enough?

If no-one else was going to repair her, she would have to make some decisions. Firstly, she realised that she would be of neither use nor interest to Neil if she became ill or stopped caring for herself. She must eat properly, clear the system with fruit and mineral water for a week, then move on to carbohydrates. She looked out an old leotard at the back of a drawer and called a leisure centre in the next town to join some classes and arrange a personal training programme. She wasn't going to go back to work, for at this greatest and most danger-ous time of her life there were more important considerations. The doctor's note was easy.

Secondly, she realised that she would need a structure to her days and an order in her home. She started cleaning. Everything. Each wooden surface, each piece of fabric, each ornament and book. To help create a rhythm to it all she started to fill the house with music from old CDs picked virtually at random. Of course, this backfired more than once as memories of shared happy moments were brought back to life, making her fall limply into a chair. But she got up again, per-severed, and on Sunday the seventeenth heard Sting tell her what she needed: "If you love somebody, set them free." Ellie stopped what she was doing as the words burned into her mind. It was the turning point.

She knew now that the letter and the flower had been mistakes, only putting more pressure on him, and she had genuinely to give him the space he'd asked for, whatever the cost. If this meant giving him up, for the sake of his peace, then she must do it though her own life be laid waste. After all, she loved him more than herself. And if one day he came back freely, she would be ready.

Yet consider this… Just how do you face the prospect of entirely giving up the dearest thing in your life, the greatest joy you have ever known and the thing that has made the whole stupid struggle worth-while? How do you risk absolutely everything, lay your life on the words of a song, on a throw of the angels' loaded dice? Ellie's mind took her back to that Saturday night when she had crept into bed beside him and felt her very spirit lift up from her body in utter freedom. This was now a matter of religion.

Valeria advertised her services in the local paper. As psychic mediums go, she was hardly an international celebrity yet her modest gifts of healing and clairvoyance were on hand only a few streets away and that seemed a good enough sign from above. Ellie had been brought up to go to Sunday School so whilst she couldn't these days claim to be religious – she would say that she believed only in right and wrong and truth – she at least had a sense of life's mysteries and was humble enough to accept that others had their alternative views. Perhaps, at a time of chaos, clearer views. Valeria may turn out to be a fraud, but she couldn't do any more damage than had already been done.

In fact she was nice, a simple and homely housewife of late middle-age who judiciously divided her time between a grumpy and demanding husband and the kinder if no less demanding spirit world. Her only concession to style was an iridescent silver scarf falling loosely around her neck. A small back room of her house was set aside for this work, holding a few pictures, books and symbolic ornaments and two comfortable armchairs beside a card table. She made no great claims of cosmic miracles or the channelling of archangels. Ellie felt at ease and, when she left, comforted. She had told Valeria only that she had 'lost someone' and was grieving. But the Tarot cannot be fooled.

"This is not someone in Spirit," intoned the woman gently, "this is a man you love." She studied the spread of cards for a long time, silently, as though trying to come to terms with an unusual intensity. At length, she had swept the cards aside into an untidy pile and reached across to take Ellie's hand. The sudden and unexpected human touch, the first in nearly three weeks, brought tears to her eyes again.

"Look, my dear, I'm speaking to you as a friend now. I think you need a friend and anyway I'm sure you wouldn't believe me if I said that your life's all mapped out and this or that is going to happen. But I do see that it's a time of crisis for you both. And a matter of faith. Of great faith.

"I can tell you this, though. It's entirely possible that you'll be together again before the moon is full. Timing is crucial here. What you desire is possible, and if it comes about then nothing will part you again. But you must wait, you must be very patient and faithful. I wonder, how good are you at those things?" There was another silence as Ellie wrestled with the question of just how patient a human being was expected to be.

"You need to understand something about men, too, my dear," Valeria continued, speaking from personal experience. "Perhaps you haven't learned yet that men are expected to be strong and brave, to be always in control. Yet they are spirits too, despite appearances at times, and as full of hopes and fears as any of us. It can be hard for them to manage all this. I think your man is also going through a tough time. I think he might be frightened, perhaps even of you, of your feelings being so strong."

Ellie sat back in surprise, pulling her hand away. Come on, afraid of love? But when she sat at home later in the evening, thinking it all through calmly, she understood. Neil's marriage was failing and he was in pain, afraid of everything going wrong and him not being strong enough to manage everybody else's needs let alone his own. Obviously he needed space and time for all these feelings to run their course and settle. He needed to feel free.

She glanced down beside her at the book she'd bought from Valeria about setting our intentions and sending them out into the universe. The plan was relatively simple, on the face of it. She would strengthen her belief by prayer. She set up a small altar in the bedroom and placed crystals and fresh white flowers on it alongside Neil's photograph. Each morning and evening she lit a blue candle, burned frankincense and prayed for his peace of mind. When she went to bed she went through their last night together in her mind, following the book's instructions on how to relax and allow her spirit to fly free of her body and to be with him in his sleep, to comfort him.

It was now Sunday the twenty-fourth of May and two and half weeks until the full moon on the tenth of June. To anyone else, this would have seemed a short time.

These last three weeks had been a blessed release for Neil. It was true that Ellie was lovely and they'd had some good times, not merely an escape from the battleground of home. Well, only at first. He did care for her and despised himself for hurting her, but then he didn't seem able to help himself causing pain one way or another. By that Sunday it had all become too much, the emotion overpowering, the fear growing. And by Tuesday he was himself again, locking it all away in the dark and private back room of his mind so that he could get on with the real world of dealing with home and work and planning a new life. He had understood what it took for her to write that letter and it was nice, but still too much. He couldn't imagine how to respond. Along with the rose he had put it in the waste bin at the edge of the car park.

Of course, she was not out of his thoughts entirely. He couldn't throw their experiences away any more than he could throw away the small photograph of her kept in the back compartment of his wallet. It had been good to see her smiling face each time he arrived on Thursdays. Her soft body pressed against his had been exciting, as were the illicit dates in the wine bar and countryside. But right now there were more immediate issues to deal with, like balancing figures, reassuring children and wondering whether and how to leave a wife of fifteen years. Maybe he should have done that earlier but he hadn't learned enough about himself yet. Yes, at least Ellie had shown him that another life was possible. She had set him free.

He was rather surprised to hear from a friend who worked at the leisure centre a few miles away that Ellie had joined and the second call a week later was more disturbing. Not only was she working out more than two hours a day, she was pushing herself far beyond the programme devised for her, driving back the limits, shaking with the exertion. It was surely too much. But she spoke to no-one, didn't acknowledge the trainers, her face a mask of determination with lips moving silently and repetitively in some personal mantra, earphones shutting out the world around. There seemed to be some kind of demon in her.

Neil was a decent enough man and felt a pang of responsibility. But no, he was not going to accept any guilt. Her life was her own affair and anyway it was good that she wanted to get in shape, be more attractive. Some other decent man would break through her barriers sooner or later, someone caring and uncomplicated. Perhaps Carl? He shuddered at a memory that he thought had been forgotten. That had hurt. He'd just needed her to be patient and faithful while he worked things out. And although he had no right to be jealous, the thought of another man entering her had raged in him. It had only been one mistake, but one too many. She had to be put out of mind.

But on Monday the twenty-fifth of May, a strange thing began to happen. At first it was so almost imperceptible that he thought little of it. You can't leave two years behind and not have stray thoughts. Yet within a few days, Neil was recognising a pattern: each morning and each evening at about the same times he would find himself thinking about her. These were not memories. He was not idly wondering how she was. It was just Ellie appearing in his mind. And if he closed his eyes he would see her face, saying nothing, simply smiling quietly at him.

He began trying to force her out by turning on the television or starting a pointless conversation with his wife and sometimes it worked. But she'd still be there when it ended, as though waiting patiently for him to give her his attention again. Then it would gently fade away until the next time. By Wednesday the third of June, more than a month after their separation and when he thought it must surely be all over, she was in his sleep too. He'd never been one to pay much attention to dreams and it wasn't as if these were dramatic and heart-racing; on the contrary, at around three-thirty each morning he would find himself half-awake, his body perfectly still, with a clear sense of having been floating above rooftops and trees with Ellie beside him and reaching out a hand. Sometimes he even seemed to see a kind of silvery haze suspended in the air of the bedroom, before normal senses took over. So he was not free after all.

Such things could have been worrying, even frightening, to some. But the strangest thing of all was that Neil felt a definite growing peacefulness that flowed slowly out into his everyday life. And within a few more days he knew how things had to be. He gave in.

He had told himself many times – and lest he forget, his friends had often reminded him – that when one relationship is in trouble the very last thing you do is start another. You need space. You need time. This is rational. But life isn't, is it? You cannot decide whom to meet and when and have it all neatly planned out. Life is messy. And if it strikes out of the blue at the wrong time, you'd better be ready or lose your chance forever.

Here was a woman with a lovely body and a gentle mind, who was always pleased to see him, who wanted to make him feel good, whose feelings had been undiminished for more than two years and, indeed, seemed to love him even more than herself. The right time or wrong, freedom or none, she was deep within him and he couldn't let her go. He no longer wanted to. Of course Ellie wasn't perfect, she had weaknesses and he got frustrated with her and they had few common interests. But now he had to face the fact that he did love her and none of those things mattered. He called her 'phone but it went to voicemail and this couldn't be left to a disembodied voice. He thought about going round but the moment never seemed right.

Then another revolution, no less, broke out. Having made a decision – at least, he believed it was his – and unlocked that dark and private room at the back of his mind, Neil released far more than his own painful memories. Some gentle yet powerful energy came too and began to change things. His wife suddenly dropped her bitter façade and wanted to talk things over, agreeing that their marriage was ending, promising to cooperate and agree terms. There would be no need for lawyers. They would share responsibility for the children. It seemed miraculous, every tension eased, the future open.

Neil had never felt so free.

Φ

Had she stopped to think about it, Ellie would have been astonished by her own self-discipline. Her skin was clear, her hair shone and her body ached with renewed energy. Her thoughts were focused and her belief total. The pain still lingered and there were a few tears at vulnerable moments, but these simply drove her perseverance. She was, after all, fighting for her life.

She had learned fast, this release of the spirit. Following the book's instructions, she had studied herself in the long mirror, become acutely aware of her breathing and heartbeat, and dissociated herself from the body, recognising that her consciousness was not located there. She had learned the techniques of relaxing quickly whilst staying alert and allowing her awareness to float freely around her room and beyond. To be honest, it was coming easily to her. The joy she had felt five weeks earlier was still within her mind and only needed a touch of thought for her whole self to become light. A universal touch.

She had continued to visit Neil each night as he slept, sensing his fears and lingering just long enough to reassure him. Then on Monday the eighth of June she wrote the whole story down so it may never be forgotten. This story.

Throughout the next day, however, she found herself suddenly and unaccountably gripped by terrifying doubt. The time was almost upon them. What if she had failed? What if she had not done enough, or too much? For a while, the tiny girl reappeared, trembling with fear and feeling very alone. On the edge. Then it was dismissed. Failure was inconceivable because this was going to be forever. On Wednesday the tenth of June she went calmly to bed like every other recent night.

Except that this time she left her body behind.

Neil arrived on Thursday just as the local doctor, grim-faced and visibly shaken, supervised the removal of the stretcher to a waiting ambulance. A small knot of neighbours slowly dispersed, muttering quietly to each other, leaving just one homely-looking, late middle-aged woman wearing a plain coat and an iridescent silver scarf. Neil stood by his car door and looked at her, transfixed by total incomprehension and unable to speak.

"You're too late, my dear," she said to him. "A day too late. The full moon was early yesterday evening. You didn't just break her heart. It was her mind."

When This Is Over

when this is over
and the dark night flies in the face of our dreams
when nothing we know
is the way that it seems now...
will the candle still burn
will your body still turn on to me
will it be
the same

when this is over
and the shadows have fled from the marketplace
where souls are sold
for a handful of warm embraces...
will that be the end
will I still call you 'lover' and 'friend'
will you be
the same

when this is over
and we finally see why it had to be...
will our spirits accept
its necessity
and in the final release
who will pick up the pieces
and be
the same

Today

bareback over broken rooftops
roughshod daybreak rides
and beckons to me
with finger shafts
so pistol straight
stealing from me
as for its very own
the words I'd saved for you

The Victim

your see-through sorrow
and your salty tears
cling on
like death's thin fingers
playing at the corners
of your tragic mouth
where
slightly parted
cusped lips of your unexplored
and lovely chasm
haunt my memories

and your rejection
lives in me
with rolling encores

Dream Catcher

The Hostess

her hand
long tapered painted sword
accepts a cigarette
and he breathes in the smoky particles
of shallow conversation

whilst deeply self-effacing
her rising breasts reach out to him
and hooded eyes
lash his desires to the oars
of hers

her tongue a longboat whip
twists lazily around the naked backs
of words
unconscious of the pain in him
just pausing every now and then to touch a lip
already moist
with confident expectancy
and dry white wine
with ice

A Tiger Outside The Gate[1]

It still upsets me to tell this story and even now I'm not sure how true it is. You may end up wondering, like me, if truth means much anyway if our everyday lives are not where we think they are, if our being is somewhere else entirely.

It had been a cool late January day in London and I was enjoying an hour in Hyde Park at lunchtime, to get some fresh air and lighten my spirits during a grey winter of frustrations at the office. I had coffee by the Serpentine and then walked beside the lake, taking in the early daffodils and the chatter of small children out with their mothers to enjoy some afternoon sunshine. I stood near the bridge to watch the light dancing on the quiet ripples of the water, tensions draining away with the normality of it all, not imagining that everything I thought I knew about being human was about to change.

---

[1]   After Neil Diamond: "…like a man with a tiger outside his gate, he not only couldn't relax but he couldn't relate…" (*Crunchy Granola Suite*)

Ironically, as it would prove, it was the man's reflection that I recognised. He was standing just a few feet away from me, staring down intently into the stillness below as though hoping to find something there. Or to lose himself.

"Joseph, my old friend!" I exclaimed, turning immediately and approaching him with a broad smile and the genuine pleasure of finding something valuable, once lost. We'd been at university together years before but almost lost touch since then except for the odd letter and an occasional drink on his rare and brief stopovers in England. Of course, I'd read his books and not just out of loyalty – the accounts of his travels in some of the world's strangest places were vivid and exciting, bringing to life the extraordinary people and customs he'd encountered. Some had said he was one of the most powerful writers of our day, renowned for his strength of character and absolute integrity.

But the man in front of me now was anything but strong. His drawn features, stooped shoulders and lethargic walk as we set off together alongside the lake suggested that Joseph was, or had recently been, very ill. Indeed, it was clear that he hadn't even recognised me at first, although after a few moments a dim light flickered in his eyes.

"Ah yes," he'd said hesitantly, "forgive me. I know your face, but… no doubt we do know each other."

I led him, almost like a child, with a soft hand at the elbow, back to the café and it didn't escape my notice that his eyes never left the water for a moment, searching beneath the wavelets. His speech was slow and his voice tired, but little by little I gained his confidence until at length he admitted, whilst he still wasn't completely sure who I was, that he felt I was indeed a friend and as such, yes, someone he could talk to. Bemused, I accepted that for the moment.

Of course, I already knew some of his back story. As students we'd been on quite different courses yet had struck up a firm friendship at one of the Saturday gigs in the Union. Well, actually the band had been so awful – I can't even remember who they were now – that we'd found ourselves together in a corner of the bar. Over many such evenings there we'd got to know one another at that deep, rather intense level that students do. His family had been more dysfunctional than most and Joseph grew up pretty much alone, a restless introvert without an identity yet with a determination to take whatever risks were necessary to find one.

That he was able then to open up to me was a special gift I should probably have appreciated more at the time, made more of an effort to stay in touch after university. But he was always going to be a loner, what the I Ching calls a Wanderer, one who is cautious of others, whose home is the road and who never lingers long in one place, like fire on a mountain.

And so he had indeed travelled in the world's most inaccessible places, blending as though invisible into its most secret societies and dark corners, and bringing them faithfully, one might say fearlessly, to light in his books so that those of us who lacked his courage and vision might come to know better our extraordinary world. Then, after many years of this inexorable travelling, he had finally found in his mid-forties what he was searching for.

Mia was twenty years younger, living in a remote South American village and clearly his soulmate. Their life together was very private and I only knew this much because there had been one interview in a Sunday travel supplement, probably at the insistence of his publisher, and the Joseph that I had known leapt out to me from between the lines. It had made me so happy to think of him at peace.

That had been no more than a couple of years ago, so what had happened to turn my brave friend into this shamble sitting beside me, withdrawn and grey? I gently prompted him with my own memories until at last he accepted, albeit apparently with reluctance, that I could be trusted.

In a low, hesitant voice that I had to lean forward to hear, he told me that he had stopped travelling for a while so as to share more time with Mia, before eventually making one last trip to the Far East to fulfil his contract with the publishers. On his return – this would have been about a year ago – Mia had been waiting for him outside the small rural airport and had raced excitedly across the dusty road to meet him. She had been killed instantly by a speeding car as Joseph watched in horror a few feet away. The driver was never traced. Which of us can begin to imagine the pain, the grief... the emptiness of life thereafter?

Checking my watch, and somehow realising the importance of this moment, I made a quick 'phone call to the office, excusing myself. Urgent personal business.

"At least," he went on after a long pause, his voice flat and matter of fact, "that's what I was told. For myself, I remember nothing about it. Nothing. When I try, all I can see is her face, laughing and happy, nothing else. I can hardly even remember anything about my life before that moment. They say I was in some kind of coma for several days. Amnesia, shock, that sort of thing. And of course they said my memory would come back gradually."

"Hasn't it?"

"No. But it's not that, it's not like they said, not amnesia. It's like I'd never existed at all before, not really, not fully. Oh, I've got my flat here in London and the books they say I wrote and some strange carvings from here and there... And sometimes people come round who say they're my friends... well, they used to until they realised I'm not good company anymore. But none of it—" he waved an arm vaguely in the air as though to indicate the whole world "—means anything. Nothing seems the least bit important. I have no way of knowing, me, personally, if I ever really did have this life they talk about. And if I did, to be honest, there doesn't seem much point in it anyway. Because..."

I waited as his eyes returned to gaze intently through the window. The shadows were beginning to lengthen now, most of the mothers and their children gone, the café's lights bobbing on the water like pale, drowned ghosts. We had already been here a couple of hours. He was beginning to withdraw again so I quietly prompted him with a hand on his arm.

"Go on, Joseph. Because of what?"

When he turned back to me I couldn't help but start. His expression was so dark as almost to have changed his very features and I'll swear the colour of his eyes was different now.

"Well, I did say that I thought I recognised you," he began, his search now transferred to my face. "But it's not from here, not in London or the university you've been talking about, not this life at all. No, I've seen you somewhere else, somewhere very different." He paused again, searching my face with those new eyes as though trying to decide who I was and whether I would just get up and leave if he continued. "There's a lot I haven't told you," he continued at last, "much more to all this… because I was hoping you'd know it without me having to say anything. But obviously you don't. So why should you believe me? They all say I've lost my mind anyway."

"Please try me," I encouraged him. "I will at least listen and I want to help if I can. Whether you believe it or not, I am your friend. So, think of me as a new friend, then." The slightest trace of a smile brushed his lips and he relaxed just a bit.

Φ

"All right, friend. It's like this. When I was in the hospital, they said I was in some kind of trance or something, maybe a coma. Lifeless.

But I was more alive then than I had ever been. That was my normal life. And that's where I remember you from. And it's continued, ever since I came round and went… well, what they said was home, here in London. I wander through the days doing this and that. Mostly, I seem to find myself drawn to water, lakes and rivers, because something hidden deep in my mind tells me… But really I'm only waiting for the night, because every time I sleep I go to the other place."

"So it's dreams?"

"You could call it that. The psych called it that. It'll do, as a word. But I've done my own research and it's nothing like how other people describe dreams."

"And what is this place you go to?"

"Just a village, in the snow. It's my home."

As the story unfolded I was gripped not just by the narrative but equally by his complete conviction, and it was one of those moments when your whole being tenses with the significance of what's happening. This wasn't just another episode from a travel book, this was my old friend – there are people who remain your true friends whether you see one another in twenty years or not, because of what you once shared – going through a personal crisis that nobody else could relate to.

Joseph's dreams, as we may as well call them, were of a small settlement apparently somewhere in the Arctic, a tiny place barely touched by civilisation where a simple, almost primordial life of fishing and hunting and the hardships of nature was lived. He himself was one of the villagers and he spent most of his time exploring alone before returning for a meal with one family or another. His own wife had been killed by a hunger-crazed white snow tiger that attacked while the men were away on a hunting expedition. That was all he knew. From the moment the dreams began, Joseph the Inuit also had almost complete amnesia of his past.

The café management, by means of that very polite and discreet way that well-trained hovering waiters have, were growing impatient with us occupying a table for so long over a couple of coffees. I ordered a light meal for us both; Joseph certainly looked in need of food, though he merely picked at it absent mindedly.

"This much," he went on, thankfully a little more animated anyway, "could be explained well enough by psychoanalysis. God knows, they've made me see enough shrinks and I'm sure you can imagine what they say. But there's another, well, another dimension to it all that no-one seems to get. These so-called dreams are consistent and continuous – when I go to sleep in London I awake there in the village and each day follows the previous one. The plans I make one day, or night, are carried out the next. And of course it's the same the other way round, when I sleep there, like I have two different and separate lives, so when I wake up there I tell them my strange dreams about a big city with people in funny clothes and animals that run on wheels... Well, I used to, they don't listen to me anymore. Two different lives and everyone thinks I'm mad in both of them..." He waved a hand in quiet despair.

"And no rest in either place," I observed. "No wonder you look so ill."

"You don't believe me, do you?" he accused, staring at me again with those strange eyes, his hands on the table as if about to rise and leave. "You think it's all my imagination too, eh? Or just another travel story."

"Come on, Joseph," I objected, "I'm not saying that at all. But it's not easy to take in. I do want to understand, to help you if I can. Look, let's walk outside for a while." He agreed readily, glad to be back by the water's edge, so I left a few notes on the table beside our unfinished meals. We paused at a bench and he accepted a cigarette from me, drawing deeply on it with obvious pleasure, the exhaled smoke drifting lazily between us on the early evening breeze. Perhaps it helped to anchor him in my world. A crispness in the air reminded me that spring was some way off yet.

"What about time?" I suggested after a while, frowning as I struggled with this nonsense, as it seemed. "That doesn't work out. I mean, if you sleep eight hours here that has to be the same as sixteen hours in… wherever it is." He shook his head and smiled at me almost pityingly.

"You're being too rational. Do you think I haven't told myself all those things? It just doesn't work like that. For one thing, my sleep is very erratic, sometimes ten or eleven hours. But it doesn't make any difference, the inconsistencies don't matter, or they don't exist. Maybe I just catch up in daydreams."

"Was that what you were doing by the lake, when I first saw you?"

"I suppose so, maybe," he shrugged. "The water seems to draw me in. I can lose myself. Rest. And there's a big lake near the village too, a strange one that never freezes over completely—" He stopped suddenly, apparently lost in thought again, but then turned to me and gripped my arm as if he'd made a decision. "I know you can help me, new friend. I'm sure of it. Look, I've tried everything else, all these pills they gave me and making myself stay awake and even memorising my old diaries, going through photographs, everything."

"So why are you so sure that I can help?" What he said next shook me rigid and changed my own life forever.

"Because you're there too. In the village. That's what I was trying to say earlier, when I said I remembered you."

He said it casually, almost as though I should have realised, and

I suppose for him it was a fact. As for me, well, in the pale light of a normal London day, I felt cold fingers of fear creep all over me.

"You live there too," he continued, "and we know each other – though we rarely speak. So you see, somehow everything would have been all right if... if you'd remembered. Well, maybe not all right but a bit easier to deal with. It would make some kind of sense because it's not just that dreams are usually incoherent or jumbled up or unrealistic, they're also private, and no-one else can have the same dream. But in ordinary life, other people see what you see and that makes it real. It's that shared awareness that makes things real. So if you'd had the same experience... But you *are* there."

His head fell into his hands and he sobbed as though his last hope had evaporated, and a small boy passing nearby with his mother looked at us with obvious surprise. Men aren't supposed to cry, he would have been told. Men have to be strong. In public anyway.

I might not have understood the story but anyone could see how real his pain was. Somehow I persuaded him to come home with me to get warm, have a proper meal and maybe to stay a while. Actually, after some initial hesitation he agreed willingly on the grounds that a different bed and surroundings might change something. I talked to him throughout that evening of the times we had spent together as students, the music and the discussions long into the night at the Union bar, the football matches we'd gone to, the girls and the parties. I even found some old photographs. But nothing brought the slightest recollection for him. It was all a total blank and I was just a village hunter who had mysteriously appeared in funny clothes in his dream of a huge city where animals run on wheels.

With some effort, I began to try to think of it from his point of view. Since the moment when his wife had been killed – by a car, or a tiger? – it seemed that here was a man with an absolutely consistent double life, albeit with the past obliterated from both. Yet I and many others knew a lot about his past in this world, at least, so it did exist because of what he'd called our shared awareness. So had he also had a complete earlier life in that other world? In other words, had he always had two lives? Perhaps that one moment of tragedy just somehow make him aware of it.

They do say that we only use a small fraction of our brains, so what's going on in the rest?

It was approaching midnight as I stood in my kitchen lost in these thoughts, almost believing him, getting drawn in too far. That would make me an Arctic villager too and the life that I was familiar with and more or less content in would become unreal. Or only partly real, if you see what I mean. I'm not sure that I do. Shaking my head to clear it, I found the room full of steam from the boiling kettle. The automatic switch had failed for some reason and in fact all sorts of appliances started acting up in the next few days. Anyway, when I took the herbal tea in to him he seemed to have suddenly brightened up.

"I've thought of a test," he said, sitting bolt upright on the edge of my sofa with a new light in his eyes. "Now that I've told you all about it, perhaps you'll be able to dream it too. I mean, perhaps you'll start remembering. If I tell you everything I know about your life there, it could trigger something… you know, like people can sometimes programme their dreams."

"Hmm," I began warily, not sure I would like what was coming. For one thing, I've always disliked snow. "What sort of thing are you thinking of?"

"Well, we could arrange to meet there, I mean one night, when we're asleep here. And if we recognise each other and remember it when we wake up, I mean here… Don't you think that would begin to make some kind of sense of everything? I know, we could go to see a film tomorrow – something not too modern or violent, maybe some kind of adventure – and see if we can discuss it in the village. Then we'll know for sure!"

It was crazy of course but he was so excited and burning with anticipation now that I had to agree. Even so, if it did work, where would that leave me?

The next eighteen hours or so were among the most bizarre of my life as he spilled out in fine detail all he knew about that other life. And despite myself I found that I was being drawn deeper and deeper into it. He was a very good story-teller, as I already knew; too late, I wished I'd switched on a tape recorder. Soon I was enveloped in his description of me as the hunter, an introspective character married to a dark, attractive girl. I wasn't even that surprised when my girlfriend Hannah called in unexpectedly the next day and Joseph immediately recognised her too. It was as though another piece of his personal jigsaw had slotted into place. But this was even more weird, since of course they had never met before. Not in England anyway.

In the end we all watched a wildlife documentary on television instead of going out for a film and at his suggestion we 'arranged' to meet at the lakeside that night. But I could barely sleep, my head too full of questions and anxieties, so I smoked one cigarette after another and imagined myself beside the Serpentine, staring deeply into the quiet water and trying to make sense of nonsense. When I looked in on him he was far away, very still and barely breathing, and in the morning he was disconsolate.

"You were there," he insisted, "but you were asleep and I couldn't wake you."

After a few days, I persuaded Joseph to come with me to see the one doctor who had shown him some sympathetic interest in the past. But the failure of our experiment, and of the others we tried, only confirmed the inevitable professional opinion.

"There's probably some element of, ah, extrasensory perception going on," the man announced, making it clear that this was a big concession, "but it will clear up given plenty of rest. Why not take a holiday, get away from it all somewhere you've never been before?" For Joseph, there weren't many such places. The doctor offered a few more platitudes and reassurances, since what is impossible may not be given space in the mind, and at the end of the day one's reputation is all one has in his world. As his pretty, young receptionist showed us out, Joseph stared intently at her, frowning, and for a moment opened his mouth to speak before thinking better of it.

We were making no progress. The more I tried to enliven his life in London and to bring him into the world I knew, the more outrageous were the dreams he reported to the villagers who now began, he said, to mock him. He withdrew further, alienated in both lives. Inevitably, a critical day had to arrive.

"There's no choice now," he said quietly over breakfast. "The doctor was right." My spoon was suspended in mid-air as I looked back at him in surprise, maybe with even a touch of disappointment too. "I should take a trip," he went on, "but not a holiday. I'm going to go and find the village. I mean, we don't even know whether it exists in this Godforsaken world but, if it does, then maybe I'll find myself too."

"But," I began, feeling excitement and relief in equal measure at the return of his bold spirit, "how can you do that? I mean, where do you start looking?" Just how does one find somewhere that exists only in the mind?

"Well, apparently I used to be a traveller, eh? So I will be again. You can help me with the research." Of course, I had to offer to go with him – it was the honourable thing to do – and was hardly able to conceal my gratitude at his refusal. I was equipped neither physically nor mentally for such hardships. And then he said something so sane, with such greater perception than anything I'd heard since that day in Hyde Park, that suddenly I felt genuine hope for him after all. "No," he said, "I have to be alone. I mean, only with people who aren't personally involved. The crew will know nothing about the real purpose of this because if it turns out somehow that I'm wrong… that I'm… well, it's just better that way."

The preparations took several months, orchestrated by his publishers who were probably surprised by his re-emergence and new interest in the frozen north yet no doubt delighted that their erstwhile profitable investment showed signs of further return. Naturally they weren't told the whole story either. But they had to be told something, some reasonable objective, for the sake of the other members of the expedition and for calculating supplies. My chief role in the venture was to build Joseph back up to physical fitness with good food and arranging an exercise regime that would have wilted many an ordinary man. But he was no ordinary man.

And now that he had a firm plan, a friend and others' support, the real Joseph was reborn. He returned to his own flat and tidied it up, spending the days while I was working with suppliers and prospective crew members. In the evenings he came back to my place where a long-suffering Hannah cooked for us all and then we spent many hours poring over travel books and recordings for clues, even though he knew the village was virtually unknown to everyone else. Then, late one night, he grabbed my arm and pointed shakily at the obscure map he'd been studying, obtained from a somewhat suspicious Russian professor of Geography at UCL.

"It's here," he whispered, "I know it is. It's not marked but I know I've heard some of these other names before. If I can just get to this town here, surely someone will know it."

I leaned over to take a look. He could certainly hardly have imagined those names nor chosen a more inhospitable region to explore. He was pointing to Verkhoyansk in Eastern Siberian Yakutia and tracing a path with his finger north-east across the Cherski range. Or should it be west over the Lena? He wasn't sure yet. The territory here was actually mapped well enough, the people of Turkic and Manchurian types rather than Inuit, yet there were indeed 'uninhabited' areas shown on the Taimyr Peninsular ten degrees within the Arctic Circle. Joseph was now confident of one thing, that in the long dark nights of these cold wastelands he would find himself.

Most of the time during this period, he had submitted fairly cheerfully to the health regime I imposed. But his mood could still swing unpredictably between determination as the plans steadily took shape and a dark, obsessive isolation. The dreams were becoming ever more vivid for him and there were days when he wasn't at all sure which world he had woken up in. And whilst I and others in London gave our care and support, he reported that he was becoming increasingly ostracised by the villagers who feared what they regarded as his madness, talking about making a trip to unknown places. Most of his time there, he said, was now spent alone on long vigils in the wastes beyond the settlement.

"What are you looking for there?" I asked him.

"The tiger," he said calmly. "It's coming back. It has to, I know it."

I hesitated quite a while before saying what had to be said next.

"Look, my friend," I began, as gently as possible, "we checked that out, didn't we? There aren't any tigers there. Reindeer and bears, yes. Maybe seals. But no tigers." He just smiled almost pityingly at me and shrugged.

"No known tigers, perhaps," he said. "But that doesn't mean they're not real does it? Besides, I only need one."

After that, there were a lot of things I'm just not sure about. If anything, this is the hardest part.

I kept in touch with the publishers but even they had almost no news because the radio links kept breaking down. The expedition returned after five months and I went to see Joseph at his flat as soon as I got the news, a couple of weeks later. He'd found the village. From the port of Khatanga, the trail led north to a place where the people had heard tell of a lake that never quite froze over, although everyone he'd spoken to just laughed at the idea of a settlement there.

"But I knew where to go anyway," he told me, "as soon as we got near. The others took some convincing but I just knew. I was coming home. All the same, we weren't welcomed at the village so we made camp a little way off and I went in alone. It was obvious they didn't want us there though they seemed, I don't know, fascinated by me, as though they recognised me. But it was difficult to communicate with them, their language wasn't anything like what we'd expected. Eventually I worked out that they were frightened because I looked so much like one of them, the mad one who spent all his time alone beyond the lake."

"But you've got some film, I suppose, and photographs?"

"They smashed up all the equipment."

He told the rest of the story flatly, without any emotion, as though whatever life had been renewed in him earlier was now drained by coming face to face with the truth. Well, he was exhausted, of course, in every sense. So he had gone out alone across the steppes to search for the outcast, a day's journey into nothingness. The rest of the crew had naturally objected to this foolhardiness, insisting that others accompanied him, but somehow he'd persuaded them by agreeing to lay a trail and carry a Lee-Enfield 7.62 rifle.

Then, looking for himself, he was nowhere, London and village alike left behind in a region where maps were useless. There had been a blizzard of freezing snow and biting, blinding winds and he'd stumbled through it, disorientated, until chancing upon a makeshift hut at the far edge of the lake. It was deserted. He'd waited there for several hours to recover some strength, before going out again to wander alongside the lake, dragging himself along as he weakened and calling out in words he didn't know. It wasn't just the physical effort now, he was close to the edge of his mind.

Just the once, a figure had loomed out of the snow mist no more than a few yards away and stared at him in shock before disappearing. Joseph couldn't say what had happened after that. A rescue party from his expedition eventually found him, collapsed and more dead than alive, but they'd got him south to a hospital of sorts and then back home. The publishers were not best pleased.

It was by now more than a year since I had chanced upon my old friend beside the Serpentine and spring was beginning to soften the air outside and lighten the days with hope. But there was no spring inside Joseph's small flat. Souvenirs and photographs of another life were thick with dust whilst maps and old newspapers all but covered the carpet. The hallway was strewn with unopened post and empty tins, packets and crockery were piled up in the kitchen. Joseph was wearing old, torn clothes, his hollow cheeks unshaven and the light of his eyes as dim as before. He was a man living entirely within his own head.

I made him some tea and got him to lie down while I tidied up a bit and went out to get some food. It was déjà vu at the kitchen table as he picked absently at what I'd prepared. Eventually, I had to break the silence.

"Was I there?" I asked. "Or Hannah? Did you show them our photographs?"

"They clearly recognised you," he nodded. "But... I don't know exactly. It seems you'd gone away somewhere."

"And the dreams? Since you got back, do you still—?"

"Of course, why wouldn't I? I just wait in the hut or walk alongside the lake. With no-one to tell my dreams to."

For a while I busied myself around the flat again, washing up and cleaning, making a shopping list, as much to stop myself thinking as anything else. I didn't know what to think. I no longer knew what to say or how to help. Then towards ten o'clock Joseph suddenly became tense again, standing up abruptly and staring around the place wildly as if searching for something before finally taking a photograph of Mia from the mantelpiece and gripping it tightly with both hands inches from his face.

"The tiger," he breathed, almost inaudibly. "It's coming back. It's hungry."

I had to leave soon afterwards – Hannah was unwell so I'd arranged to call in – but I calmed Joseph down as best I could and promised to return the next day. But I never saw Joseph again.

A neighbour told me that she'd heard a loud, strange cry and some foreign words later that night. She'd gone to her front window and seen Joseph walk quite deliberately from the front door and out into the path of a passing car. Neither the driver nor Joseph stood any chance.

And were this the end of the story it would be enough, complete at least for those who believe in everyday reality. But a few weeks later I decided to visit the doctor I'd gone to with Joseph that time before. I suppose I needed to try to understand a few things better; and for all that he had failed to help then, he had seemed to be the only one prepared to accept what Joseph said to some extent at least. I know that area fairly well since it's not far from my own home and I found the address easily, only to see that workmen were busy replastering bare, empty rooms. My questions met with suspicious looks from them.

"There ain't no doctor here," one of them said at last. "Never 'as been. It's bin empty at least two year, well, 'cept for squatters. Any road, it were an office before that, some sort o' publisher or other."

I suppose I might have made a mistake with the address. That's the rational thing to say. But then I started to have strange dreams too and Hannah's losing patience with me, says I'm taking my sadness about Joseph too far. I can't seem to make her understand that they're as real as here and now, the people as solid as her, except that I'm living in a small isolated village in the foothills of the Himalayas. The frozen peaks tower over us on three sides and at night around the fire they tell stories about a rogue snow leopard.

What disturbs me most is... well, it's not that I may really be someone else on the other side of the world. Or even of another world. I'm just afraid that, having fallen asleep tonight, I may not wake up anywhere.

Yesterday, Upon The Stair

The girl is wearing a rich brown leather jacket loosely belted through a large, square brass buckle that rests in her lap. She sits upright at the far end of the carriage, right leg crossed over left, slightly flared pale blue jeans almost hiding the brown canvas shoes. From our position, her face is obscured by dark waves of hair that fall around her shoulders as she looks down, chin buried in the roll neck of her sweater, while a slender finger traces roads on a map. Then she glances up briefly at the Underground chart above the window opposite. We observe her closely because her role is important.

The train sways and people nearby tighten their grip on the poles. Through the window we see blackness rushing past us as though escaping from somewhere, then suddenly it succeeds and there's a glare of lights and a blur of advertisements until we slow and can make out the clumps of people and Belsize Park signs.

The train doors slide and the shuffling crowd leaves, following one another meekly along the platform, up the stairs and round to the lifts where someone jabs repeatedly at the call button and mutters about having to wait. The girl enters a little ahead of us and we're just able to keep her in view, careful to keep the flat brown paper package under one arm away from jostling bodies as the lift dives up. She's quite close now but turned the other way and we still can't see her face properly until we're outside on the station steps and she stops suddenly to study her map so of course we can't help gently bumping into her.

She turns to apologise and now we are looking straight into her wide grey eyes, edged with long black lashes that deepen the pupils. Close up and in sharp focus, her clear skin ebbs from high cheekbones that carry no make-up at all, taut from her small, straight nose, to settle warmly around a self-deprecating smile.

"I'm so sorry – I shouldn't have stopped there, should I?" There's a brief pause while she looks over her shoulder towards the street. "I don't suppose… um, I mean, do you know this area, please? I want this road here." There's a red ink mark on her map.

"Sure." And we point out the turnings for her, feeling self-conscious that the skin of our forefinger is paint-stained and so much older than hers. "Right here… right… left at the bottom of the hill… over the bridge by the station… just keep going right."

Why do we not just tell her now? Something holds us back as though the story is not yet inevitable, however much we know it to be so. Her soft and manicured finger is a fraction away as she follows the route and it would be so easy to touch. Sometimes things do happen as suddenly as that. It's chance. You're going about your day, feeling rather lost, and then someone walks into your life asking for directions.

"Got it. Thank you."

And she's gone, swinging into the early evening with hands thrust into pockets and shoulder bag gripped between arm and body. We watch for a few moments then we're on the pavement buying a newspaper from Jonnie at the kiosk that's been there forever. He nods a greeting and then we put our head down against the slight drizzle that's started as we turn left down the hill and then left again.

A few minutes later we're on the white stone bridge over the railway lines and the lower fields of Parliament Hill have come into view where there's a couple walking their dog, a young Labrador. A small girl swings silently in the playground to our right, long hair streaming behind her as she flies forward. She is wearing a brown jacket, blue jeans and bright red trainers. She sees us watching and stops suddenly, turning to look straight at us and smiling trustfully before kicking her feet down and away again. We go left into the road, our pale shadow from the streetlamp that's just come on racing ahead of us across the glistening wet leaves that carpet the pavement.

The gate unlatched, the key turned in the lock, we're in the hallway closing the door and noticing the green linoleum and musty wallpaper even though they're so familiar. There's a long white envelope in the wire mesh box on the back of the door so we take it out and read the printed address upside down before tearing the envelope open with the door key. We have paused to read the letter – or perhaps because we know she's nearly here – on the fifth stair when the doorbell rings.

"Hello, I wonder if – oh, it's you," she says with evident surprise. "How… I mean, how did you get here ahead of me?"

"A different way," we say simply. "Shorter but more complicated. Didn't know you were coming here."

"No, of course. Well, I'm Mrs D… the landlady, I'm her niece. It's a, you know, duty visit."

"She'll be out, always is at this time. Her door's there at the end of the hall. You'll find the key at the side, under the plant pot."

She closes the door and walks briskly along the shadowed passage as we come back down to pick up our parcel, having left it on the hall table, before starting back up the stairs again reading the letter. As we hesitate near the top she reappears below us and stands with arms clasped, shivering.

"Found it," she calls up. "You know, it's colder in here than outside. I'll see if I can find the kettle. I think I know how they work. Some tea?" Her voice is bright and friendly and she's watching us with those clear eyes that see things others can't.

The hand holding the letter drops to our side and we look back showing no sign of reaction. It's just because her features are haunting, she's young and happy, and things are happening on the inside of another life. We can hear the muffled ring of a telephone somewhere under a pillow, followed by a distant ambulance siren as a baby cries and a Yorkshire terrier scampers across a spring garden after a red ball. She cocks her head on one side in amusement and we feel a shock as though we're in a lift that has started to accelerate sideways so for a moment she goes out of focus.

"Would you like some tea?"

A cloud passes overhead.

"Sorry?"

"Yesterday upon the stair I met a man who wasn't there."

"What?"

"Lewis Carroll, I think."

We turn away and start up again because there are things to do and there's time to pass. This isn't going well, all the pieces seem to be there but we can't yet connect them. We don't mean to be rude, it just seems impossible. Instead, we pause at the top and call back to her.

"William Hughes Mearns."

"Oh well."

From the old armchair near the door we look out across the length of the studio through the wide window opposite that reaches right up to the decorative cornice below the ceiling and almost the whole width of the room. The sky is dark grey and moody now above the chimney stacks perched on the Victorian slated roofs of the terraces that back onto the railway lines. The chair is low so we can only see part of the upper floors opposite where there are yellowish lights in one or two rain-streaked windows. It's very quiet. We know how the sky feels as we glance around at this dull, untidy room and its aged, peeling paper and foot-worn grey carpet, for all the world looking like it's been empty of life for years. Yet there are canvases stacked to one side and propped against the marble fireplace to the left, blocked off because the chimney hasn't been swept for generations. An easel standing on a dustsheet smeared with paint is almost the only colour. On the small oak table beside it is a palette and a jumble of brushes in a dirty glass jar. To the right, passing the window again without noticing it, we take in the single bed pushed into one corner, the brown paper parcel now lying on its unmade sheets.

We look down at our right arm resting on the chair arm and across the patchwork of lentigines on the hand to fingers loosely gripping an untipped cigarette whose ash is almost an inch long and drooping. A mug of tea with thin floating skin sits on the printed letter on a table to one side, the paper now stained with brown rings and splashes. There's a light knock on the door. We don't move. It comes again and the door opens a fraction, stops, then a little further. So there's nothing we can do about it after all.

"Hello? I thought this must be your room – there's a light under the door. You don't mind...?" Her voice trails off as we glance up but don't answer. It isn't that we don't want to. Anyway, it doesn't matter because she has advanced into the centre of the room looking out towards the window before turning on a heel and taking in the surroundings. The room has become an open, gently sloping ploughed field and in the distance we can hear sheep and the early morning chatter of birds, before her voice intercedes and the earth is absorbed back into her. She is still wearing the jacket with arms clasped.

"My aunt isn't back and the kettle doesn't seem to work. It's freezing down there. Am I disturbing you?" That has no answer either. She swivels a little and her eyes settle on the backs of canvases. "You're an artist, then?"

"Some say so." It's the first time we've spoken for ages and it comes out awkwardly, as though from someone else, and she seems to be considering that as she moves over to the easel to study the outline of the rectangular canvas beneath its cloth cover. Gratifyingly, she makes no move to lift the cloth as many would.

"I'm just making conversation, you know. You don't mind a poor country girl turned student all alone in a strange, cold house, do you?" she says over her shoulder. It is remarkable, this refusal to be put off by our distance.

"Of course not. My mind was… far away. And I'm not used to…"

"People? Yes, I can tell. Can I sit down?" She doesn't expect an answer and because there aren't any more chairs she goes over to the bed, carefully moves the package aside and sits with a pillow at her back against the wall. "This must be a painting, then, or a print," she says, lightly fingering the brown wrapping. "Do you buy other people's work?"

"One of mine. I took it to a client."

"No joy, then?"

"Uh?"

"Well, you brought it back. Was the tint of the sunset not quite right, or has their rent gone up? That's what people say, I suppose. Did you drop the price?"

"I'd have paid them to take it. But nobody wants abstracts now. Simple as that."

"So why do you do it, I mean, if nobody…?"

She doesn't finish the question. So she is sensitive enough to realise its pointlessness and respect our disappointment at being of a different age. Many people have asked that, of course, and usually with undisguised disdain. Why write songs that will never be performed? Why write stories when people want novels? It's a sensible question for those who inhabit a sensible world.

But she's here now so we feel we need to respond, mumbling something about it being all we know how to do and about how when we look out at the world we don't see houses with house shapes and people with people shapes and landscapes with hill shapes and tree shapes. These things are only in the mind. We had to learn the techniques once but they stopped making sense because we see something else beyond… We stop because she probably thinks this is pretentious nonsense. But she's kind enough not to say so and instead asks what on earth we live on.

"Expectations of the future. And illustrating children's books. It's a specialist publisher." We point to a shelf above the bed and she reaches up to take one of the books, leafing through it quickly yet with observant eyes and interest.

"You don't like children much, do you? The monsters are drawn much better than the other characters. Brill detail."

This prompts us to suggest that monsters are simply more interesting and that she's quite wrong about the children. And suddenly we realise that we've engaged with her and have begun to accept this, so we say we'll make us both some tea. In one corner there's a small basin and some wall shelves with a kettle plugged in near the mirror; it's freestanding and we can adjust it slightly to watch her as she gets up and wanders over to one of the stacks, turning round the top canvas to study it closely. This is acceptable since it wasn't covered.

"I've never understood abstracts. This bit here – it looks like you threw your brush at it."

"You understand perfectly, then. I did. I was angry, trying to capture something in my head that didn't want to be found. Anyway, you're not supposed to find any deliberate meaning in it. That's the point, it doesn't mean anything, not in the usual sense. This kind of work is suggestive, a starting point to lead you within your own thought so that—"

"The kettle's boiling."

The rising steam is clouding her image but cannot obscure the curious smile and bright eyes. The cloud grows white and cumulus and hovers over a small boy in a red and white striped football jersey with a white ball under one arm and a lopsided grin as though in a family photograph. There are light footsteps, the brush of an arm and the click of a switch. Slender fingers holding a tea towel reach across in front of us to wipe out the boy, replacing him with a grinning girl.

"Are you all right? You don't seem altogether with it this evening."

"Not all together, no."

"It's a good job I'm not easily put off, then. And that I really need a hot drink."

Yes, it is. We move the small table and chair a little closer to the bed – only a little – then make the tea and carry two mugs over, returning with the cold one to pour away in the basin. It leaves a light brown stain. We mutter something about it being a difficult day, crowds, client, rejection letter, alienation… She picks up the envelope tossed aside when we came in.

"Mr Donald Marks. Pleased to meet you, Mr Marks. It's exciting to meet someone who's going to be famous one day. Oh, don't ask how I know, I'm just intuitive like that. And by the way, I'm Claire. Mrs D was my father's brother's… um, second wife. I think. Relationships are always so difficult to work out, aren't they?" The words are falling over each other as though a simple exchange of names has exposed an intimacy that makes her nervous. "I'm down to the big scary city from the backwoods of Oxfordshire to learn some history and philosophy. UCL, first year. Seems silly, doesn't it, coming here from Oxford but I'm afraid they wouldn't have me. Their loss, Dad says. But actually—" she leans forward confidentially, lowering her voice "—I'm not really very bright. Only just scraped in 'cause the tutor who interviewed me was a big softie. And running late."

She puts her mug down and stands to take off her jacket and as she turns sideways we see the slimness of her body arched slightly against the window despite it being almost lost in the folds of the grey woollen sweater. She tosses her hair back to free it and finally settles back to perch on the edge of the bed.

"And you, famous future artist Marks? What's your story? There must be one. I'd say you're about forty though I'm no good with ages." That's true. We don't answer at first. The room needs some silence to allow it to settle again. Then we decide to try beginning.

"I'm from Oxfordshire too. Actually, it's very close to—"

"Good heavens, will you look at that!" She's pointing towards the window and instinctively we hover in our chair, leaning forward to look. "No, don't get up. Over there, the house opposite with the green curtains. You'd think they'd pull them."

Across the railway, the upstairs window is bright against the darkening evening and the two figures can be seen clearly. It's nothing. The woman has her back to us with the zip of her royal blue dress open and his hands are slipping the soft material slowly over her pale skin, down her arms and away. She stands motionless and naked, framed in the window, as the hands begin to explore. We shrug and settle back into the armchair.

"It's nothing. It's normal life, even if he isn't her husband. You see everything across the tracks and nobody minds, everybody watches everybody else. Real life isn't polite."

"Well, you wouldn't see that back home." She's still watching, fascinated.

"Only because you have net curtains."

We're a little disappointed in her now, for being naïve, inexperienced, but then she's only – what? nineteen at most. She hasn't seen any real life yet but we hold back from saying any of this. Instead, we reach with one hand to play with the corner of the cloth covering the easel as though to remove it and show her. But we hold back from that too.

"Life isn't pretty, like the fields and woods of the countryside. People struggle. The animals in the woods struggle too. Everyone's in some kind of pain, so they grab whatever happiness they can. Cruelty has to be taken for granted."

"Well, I didn't expect a philosophy tutorial this afternoon." She stands abruptly now and we automatically get up too, taking a step back as she wraps herself again in her jacket. "And by the way, this is imitation. I'm vegetarian. That's all right, isn't it? I think I heard the door downstairs so I'd better go and see if my aunt is back."

But then she hesitates and turns back, standing close and putting an arm through ours. Remarkable.

"That's why you paint, then. Because of the pain." Remarkable.

In the sudden silence of her leaving, an ache enters to fill the void of the room. Did we lose the chance? Perhaps we said the wrong thing… or didn't say… After a few moments of stillness we lift the cloth from the painting we started yesterday and slowly pour the remains of the girl's tea over it so that it streaks from the top edge and becomes a sticky mirror in which we can just make out a laughing woman holding a green curtain across her body.

"Come again, child," we think, in a whisper.

We reach the top of the white stone bridge and hesitate for a moment to look out over the playground. It is bright and sunny although there's a chill autumn breeze, and ten or so children are racing excitedly between swings and slides to keep warm, laughing and shouting while their mothers sit among shopping bags near the painted wooden gate. It is a scene of normality and hope for the future. Then there is the sound of feet running lightly up the steps behind us and a voice.

The Bridge

"Hey!" Her breath is short as she reaches our side. "Hello, it's me. Guess what, I found your shortcut."

"Claire. Visiting your aunt?" She looks at her feet a little sheepishly.

"Sort of. Though I was wondering… I mean, I thought you might be in. Working." This makes us feel good though we say nothing for the moment, looking out and away again.

"Do you see that girl? There, on the top of the slide, she's looking this way. Long hair. She's here every day on her own. That must have been you, what, twelve years ago." She follows our gaze, screwing up her eyes against the low afternoon sun before turning back to look straight at us with a blend of curiosity, concern and humour.

"There's no-one on the slide."

"Oh, she must have gone, then. But she's always there. Are you coming in for some tea?" We bend to pick up the two large tins of emulsion by our feet. "I got these for the room." And we start down the other side of the bridge and turn left.

"You're decorating? Good, about time. Why now?"

"After you came the other day." This doesn't really answer her question because we're not sure how to do that. It's just inevitable. One of those jobs that seems like a good idea and you start off full of enthusiasm and a few days later wonder why you ever thought of it because there's so much work involved and you ought to be doing other things. But you do it simply because there's an imperative to bring something new into your life. Colour. Or contrast. Or hope. It's an act of faith, to change the environment and trust that life will imitate art. She has come back, after all. "I don't know what colour it will end up as." She looks at us with a mock derogatory face, corners of the mouth down-turned and eyebrows up like a clown.

"I see. That's perfectly clear. Decided to be obtuse today, have we? I'll soon tell you what colours you need." We've reached the gate and she swings in front of us as though to bar the way. "Let's go for a walk on the Heath. It's a lovely day."

"Later. I have to take these in and I need a warm drink." We have to be inside now. We know what's happening and it has to be inside. "We'll go later and you can play on the swings. I'll push."

Φ

It is maybe three weeks later. The door looms up and the heavy old key rattles in the lock and the sunlight from across the tracks is almost violent against the shadows of the landing we're leaving so we have to hesitate before stepping through, eyes hurting and thoughts reforming. This isn't easy. We are carrying another heavy tin so we make our feet move forward and put it down beside the small table which is now central with the other sparse furniture moved away from the walls. The easel remains where it was though with a different board on it, turned towards the window. Claire has already gone to the shelf and filled the kettle before turning to look carefully, as she always does, at my small area of chaos. The wall near the bed now has broad lilac and dark blue stripes.

"I thought you'd go for pale colours, you know, for the light."

"It was a strong feeling," we say, with a flicker of worry. "I can change it if you don't like it."

"Don't be silly. You mustn't change anything for me. It's your room."

We turn to her with words half-formed but how can we say it? How can we say that the room means nothing and that everything has to change and that it is for her? She sees something in our eyes, though, and now walks slowly over to stand very close and look into them. There is deep silence. So she knows it too.

125

"Why me?" she asks, so we put our fingers lightly – ever so lightly – on her shoulders.

"You are… an echo," we say. "And there should be sound here."

Then we can feel her breath as her face turns up and comes as close as it ever could and all we can see is the grey of her eyes before they blink, and close, and there is complete darkness broken only by the rushing of a train beyond the window. Her hair touches our cheek and we can almost feel it. There's a charge of some kind of unknown energy dimly flashing far away inside us that pulls us back, back closer, so we begin to sense the aura of her body pressing itself to us as though gently pushing against the broken, old wooden door of an abandoned house.

"The kettle," she says, and pulls away.

We watch her becoming lost in a cloud of steam that fills the corner of the room and then we're driving into fog and leaning forward on our seat to peer through a murky windscreen, barely able to make out the broken white line beneath the lamps. Yellow headlights tear past the other way and all in a moment the white ball is rolling in front of us and a small boy in a red and white striped jersey is running into view from the left and stooping to pick it up, freezing there and looking right into our eyes. This is stupid. What is he doing in this room? The brakes scream.

Claire walks back out of the darkness with two mugs and we take one automatically as she moves to put hers on the table then round to the other side of the easel. It's a lightly shaded charcoal face on paper clipped to the board, though the portrait is superimposed on a kneeling male figure.

"It's me!" she says with evident surprise, leaning in to study the lines. "I'm honoured. And actually it's rather good. I can't quite make out the man, though." We do that thing again of beginning to open our mouth but the words have so far to travel we're too late. "Oh, this reminds me. I meant to tell you. I was in South Ken the other day, no, yesterday, and there was this small antiques shop, well, more bric-a-brac I suppose. Anyway, they had some paintings in the window and one was a landscape in a posh gold leaf frame. I noticed it really because it was of the Heath, not far from here. I recognised the pond, just where we were walking the other afternoon, you know, when you said it was getting cold because the sun was dying… Anyway, then I noticed the signature in the bottom corner—" there's nothing we can do to stop this now "—was Marks, the same name as you. Isn't that weird? So of course I had to go inside and the man said he thought it was late nineteenth century. But he didn't seem to know much about it actually so I don't know how he expects to sell it. And he wanted five hundred for it."

That's ironic.

Φ

Even the hardiest locals are not braving the swimming pond today but, as everyone does, we stop to lean on the wooden rail and watch the water. It's fringed with trees whose leaves have been falling for a few weeks now and a russet carpet is beginning to drift around the edges, home for the moment to thousands of jumping insects. We see them in sharp focus, the last of the day's sunshine bouncing from their black bodies and lacy wings. Before Claire came, we would not even have noticed the trees.

"Will you let me paint you? I've never done a portrait, not properly."

"Improperly, then?" I'm still never sure when she's teasing. She doesn't seem to take anything very seriously, though on balance that's probably a good thing at the moment.

"What I meant was just doing the face, nothing else, as it really is. Well, as others see it."

127

"That's it, though, isn't it?" she counters, linking her arm in ours and shivering. She's thinking that she's a step ahead but hasn't yet understood the significance of our suggestion. "What people see in a face isn't what's real. Not entirely, and not at all for you, I imagine. I mean, if you want a souvenir of someone you can just take a good photograph and..." Her voice trails off as she thinks of somewhere else in her life at some other time. "Anyway, no-one's really interested in portraits, are they, and my face is pretty ordinary. You should see some of the other girls at uni, there are plenty of beautiful people around. But faces don't tell you much these days." I suspect she may be angling for a compliment but that's not how this is going to work.

"All right, but—"

"I was in a film recently, some TV news item about students away from home for the first time. Guess what part I played?" She doesn't wait for my answer since hers is already prepared. "A bum. That's me. There was just this shot of me crossing the road and they zoomed in on my bum. I was wearing tight yellow jeans as it happens. But that's what people see, that's all I am, and if that's what you want then 'no'."

She takes her arm away and turns her back, walking slowly along the perimeter path. There is a moment of pure horror as our vision darkens and everything is out of focus because we can't see why she's upset. It has to be something from that other time.

"Claire, child," we call after her, "it's not like that..." But we're not good at explaining things and, well, even if we could, how would anyone understand? How could she accept it? In any case, she's turned sharply on her heels now and marches right up to us with a tear at the corner of an angry eye.

"Don't ever," she says coldly to our face, "call me 'child' again."

Then she's away, running with hands thrust into the pockets of the brown jacket, her head down and shrouded by tumbling hair. In the still afternoon, sounds rise up to bombard us and then fall away to nothingness. We grip the rail, clenched fingers white, because we don't feel steady as we watch her accelerating away into nowhere, although maybe it's we who are disappearing. Having come so far, surely it's not lost now? In a few minutes the mind clears and we set off back to the house.

The studio door is open and only needs a light push, and now the sun is down it's easier to move into the familiar shadows. She's sitting on the bed with her head in her hands, jacket and shoes strewn across the floor, and when she looks up we see the tears now drying in streaks on a face that glows with life. We are holding back, afraid of hurting her. Yet somehow she knows that it's up to her now, and we can hardly believe how blessed we are.

"Sorry," she whispers, "it's all right, really. Only… everything is so fast. I don't understand this and I'm always being told, every day, that I have to understand. All my life they've been saying that yet I know there are things you're not meant to understand. I do. It's like you said, about the art. But it's hard to take it all in." She stands up and goes to the window as though looking for an answer across the tracks but the sky's as grey as her eyes and as empty of suggestion as the space between us. When she turns round we take our first step into the room, leaving the door open.

"I do trust you," she continues quietly, biting her lip. "And I do want you to paint me. But not a face. And if it's to mean anything, it has to be your way. And it has to be all of me."

She's wearing a short jersey dress, chocolate brown, with a wide scooped neck that shows the pale bones of her shoulders and a loose belt of plaited, dark golden cord. Self-consciously, a little awkwardly – as though to show us that this is not a practised scene – she unties the belt and lets it fall before with alternate hands pulling the dress down over her arms so that it rests in folds about her hips like rich, ploughed earth. She is so slim, her skin is so white, her breasts so small, that we wonder how there can be so much life in her.

We take off our own jacket and hang it on the back of the chair before approaching her very slowly, aware that we are trembling with a feeling we thought lost and far away but now rushing back within and around every cell, a soft morning tide rippling over stones.

"All of me," she repeats. "And don't close the curtains."

We sit on a wooden bench overlooking the lower fields of the Heath with Claire at the other end, in profile, trying to look serious as we rough in the lines of her face on a sketchpad balanced on one knee. The painting is going to take several studies before we can capture whatever it is in our head that needs to be found, that elusive, unique facet of her spirit. As we work, the second movement of Dvořák's Ninth Symphony is heard, played in Glen Miller style by a big band, yet mellow, until orchestration gradually emerges led by a blues guitar. The mood is broken as a white ball rolls past and she jumps up and stoops to retrieve it.

She sits back down but our vision has misted over now and we're in the car again, eyes straining forward as hands wrench the wheel until we skid back into sunlight and see her fussing over the young black dog that was chasing the ball. We try to resume sketching but she decides that the moment has passed – it will always be she who decides – and she stands up reaching out an arm so that we have no choice but to take her hand and follow down the slope to the play-ground where she sits on a swing, her head right back and upside down, mouthing something to us. Obligingly, we take up our position and then there she is swinging up and away from us with legs straight out in front of her.

Back in the studio, we are mounting the stepladder on the top platform of which is a small tin of white paint that we begin to apply with a one-inch brush on top of the stripes with careful sweeping strokes. Hearing her laugh, we look down and see her pointing to the window then bending over and slapping her thighs helplessly. She is wearing our spare blue overalls, far too big for her, and her hair is tied back either side in two ponytails.

Another time, we find ourselves trapped within a crowd of people with shopping baskets and pushchairs on the far pavement from the Underground station, trying to keep up with her moving fast to our left. When she disappears from view we feel isolated and vulnerable in this incomprehensible surge and stand still, watching wide-eyed as a small family of red buses crawls past, two large ones and a small one taking up the rear. Suddenly, a half-peeled banana appears in front of our face so close that have to bite it and there she is again, smiling, with brown paper bags in her arms.

The next thing is that we're holding the bags and sitting in a cool, shaded boutique beside the long, furled beige curtains of a cubicle. The lower half of a slim leg appears around the edge of the curtain, toes pointing down stylistically, and the leg extends further to reveal her thigh before the curtain is suddenly pulled aside and she lets go of the gathered long white evening gown she's trying on so that it tumbles gracefully to cover her again. She grins modestly and steps out to swirl on the spot for us. The dress is almost backless and cut straight, a low vee-line at the front with fine, pale gold stitching at the edge. Seeing that we are mesmerised, she looks down shyly and puts one finger to her mouth. But seeing her like this was always going to mist our vision and we know by now that whenever there is mist we will see the boy in the red and white jersey, and sure enough he is there prone at her feet and a bloodstain is spreading slowly along the lower hem of the dress.

"Where do you go?" she asks gently. "Sometimes I lose you completely."

Her brown jacket is hanging over the back of the chair in the studio where she sits with blue sweater and jeans, a copy of Russell's History of Western Philosophy in her lap. We don't answer. We don't know. We look down and continue to shade in around the eyes.

In the evening, we walk together slowly in the small gallery on Heath Street where there's a solo exhibition of modern London city-scapes, and we comment on the brushwork and false shadow while she picks out the appealing landmarks that she hasn't visited yet. Then we sit by candlelight in a quiet, almost empty Chinese restaurant with garish red walls and Tang Dynasty prints by Lu Yanshao. She's holding her chopsticks in the air and has her mouth full, trying not to laugh because we've dropped our food on the white cloth.

In the morning, her soft hair is spread across the white pillow, her face lightly flushed with eyes peacefully closed as we watch her in complete silence. She is not really asleep and can always feel our look, and now she feigns restlessness so that the sheet ruffles and is pulled away from her body. A small smile plays around her lips. She knows very well that we can't take our eyes off her as we back slowly away towards the corner of the studio, where finally we splash water on our face and quietly fill the kettle.

We pick up the palette and a fine brush, crossing to stoop beside the bed where we lightly paint a few small grey tears on her cheeks and a yellow star on her forehead. Her nose wrinkles but she's still pretending to be asleep and we return to switch off the kettle before the steam can cloud the mirror. The silence is broken suddenly by the noise of a train rushing beyond the window so now she stands up, gathering the sheet about her.

"That's not what I meant when I said you could paint me."

She comes over to stand beside us at the easel where her painting is taking shape on a large landscape canvas. It is still only roughed in but there are areas of pale coral skin and a light background suggesting water and trees whose leaves form a drifting russet carpet.

"You're not supposed to see it until it's finished," we chastise gently. "It's bad luck." It is, too.

"It will be lovely," she says very quietly. "Thank you for this. I'm glad I… I mean, we… well, I was more than a bit nervous. I couldn't believe…" We understand, because we couldn't either. "It is working, isn't it," she goes on, looking up to us seriously, "for you? All the pain, the confusion… Things aren't so abstract now, are they? You can start to forget all that, can't you?" As though to emphasise her meaning, she moves closer and opens the bed sheet to wrap us both within it.

"Forget?" we say brightly, in surprise. But then, perhaps she could never really know where we come from. "Quite the opposite. It's wonderful to begin to remember everything, to begin to find the sense of it all. Yes, it's remembering. Things are clearing, nearly back where they should have been. When the painting's finished, in the New Year, we'll know what it means. Just a few more sittings and then—"

We break off because we feel her body tense against ours, her quiet energy pulling away even though she hasn't moved. And it is here, like this, when we are as close as we have ever been, and now, at the most critical point of the story, she delivers her blow with such sweet and complete surprise that it is several minutes before we realise that the words have pierced our mind and the bleeding has begun.

"You can do the rest without me, can't you?" It's a matter of fact statement. "After all, you know me well enough by now, surely. I was going to tell you before, but…" She leans her head into our shoulder as though unable to look us in the eye. "I'm not going to come for a while. See, I've got exams soon, they're really important – to check that we've all settled in and if we don't pass… And I'm way behind. Um, that's your fault. Anyway, I've got to concentrate on… so I'm going away. Home. I can work there."

Four weeks, she says. Maybe more. She'll be straight round afterwards, she says. She says she's sorry but this is her life too. We say nothing because we know we can't make demands and that she has to be free. That's rather the whole point of her. In any case, she's made up her mind.

It's only when the door has closed behind her ten silent minutes later and we've allowed another couple of minutes for her to leave the building and turn away along the pavement, that the screaming in our head begins about not being strong enough yet, about not being able to take the last step, around the corner, on the bridge that she's now crossing.

Φ

We are disengaged now and our perspective is all different, from an angle and in monochrome. Stooped slightly at the easel, wearing the same blue overalls she had worn, we work as though possessed with discarded brushes falling to the floor. One canvas is lifted off unceremoniously and leaned against a wall to be replaced by another, which receives a few cursory rapid strokes before also being replaced, and so it goes with four or five pieces rotating. An observer might consider this insensitive but we know what we're doing.

In a while – no-one can say how long – we cross the white stone bridge again with only the merest glance towards the playground and on to the Underground station. At the other end there's a large, coldly decorated office where we sit across the mahogany desk from a short, fat man who would be comical were it not for his influence. He looks over the top of steel-rimmed glasses and nods a bulbous head in and out of a grotesque double chin that folds over the white collar of his shirt as he pushes a piece of paper across to us. We pick up the pen beside it and it feels as heavy as an old iron jail key when we sign at the bottom.

Back in the crowded train compartment, the girl is sitting in the same seat but wearing a darker, more formal jacket. She rises to leave among all the others and a mass of closely packed bodies flows slowly along the platform, up and around towards the lifts. She turns left, crosses the bridge, left again and through the gate that's been left open, having to wait because there's no answer to the bell she presses so she has to press the other, lower one. Before long, a middle-aged woman opens the door and smiles to her while we take up a position behind her and halfway up the stairs.

"So, are the exams all finished now?" asks Mrs D. "Did they go well?"

"Yes, fine thanks, Auntie. I think I scraped through for now."

"I knew you would. Well, come in and tell me all about it. And what was it like being back home – are your parents all right?"

"Yes, everything's okay. Look, you go ahead, I'll just pop upstairs for a minute to see Don and then—" She stops, seeing her aunt's expression.

"What do you mean, dear? There's no-one upstairs."

"Well… I mean, Mr Marks, on the first floor. The artist."

"Where did you get that idea, Claire? There hasn't been anyone—"

But she has already pushed past her aunt and run quickly up the stairs, along the short dark passageway and into the unlocked room. It is shabby and bare except for a basin in one corner next to some empty shelves, an old mattress against one wall and a paint-streaked dustsheet lying crumpled near the window. She crosses the room slowly and looks out at the windows of houses across the tracks as though expecting someone there to give her a sign.

Back downstairs in the brightly lit kitchen, the girl is sitting at the pine table with head in hands, a mug of tea with thin, floating skin near her right elbow as slender fingers with vermillion nails grip an untipped cigarette whose ash is an inch long and drooping. Leaning against the cooker, her aunt watches silently but anyone can read her thoughts like they're in a balloon above her head. 'Working too hard… so much pressure these days…' That sort of thing. The girl lets the cigarette fall into the ash tray and absent mindedly turns the pages of the evening paper that had been left open on the table when she arrived. Suddenly she is attentive, upright with back rigid, a finger pointing to the foot of the page.

"Look, I told you, Auntie," she says. "See here… there's this gallery in Ebury Street. 'A new exhibition of the tragic artist, Donald Marks.' Opening Wednesday. I don't understand, he must have known about this for ages…"

Φ

A small, fat man with steel-rimmed glasses is hovering just inside the doors of the gallery, wearing a black dress suit and a fixed welcome expression and doing a lot of nodding towards people as they enter. The slightest trace of a frown creases his eyes as Claire enters, wearing a blue denim jacket over a short lilac skirt and clearly without the kind of lifestyle and bank account of the other evening suited patrons. There are glossy exhibition brochures on a green baize-covered table to one side, next to which a waitress in starched white offers glasses of wine and orange juice from a large silver tray. She is a student needing the money and instantly recognises Claire as a fellow being, smiling warmly while raising one inquisitive eyebrow, wondering why she's here. Others turn, with more judgemental eyebrows, but she doesn't care.

It's a long, open plan room half-filled at the moment by these twenty or so others who are mingling conversationally and paying scant attention to the art hung on every wall. Most of this is abstract, with savage colours in bold, interlocking streaks, and in some places you might think the artist had thrown his brush at the canvas. Such forms as are discernible within the chaos are probably feminine though not at all geometric. They put one in mind, perhaps, of Osnat Tzadok. However, reading the brief biographical notes printed on white card beside each piece, Claire sees that this work predates hers by almost a century and was therefore unsurprisingly rejected in its day.

Moving along to the furthest area of the gallery, it becomes evident that the artist did attempt a kind of compromise at some point as a handful of small studies are grouped together, all suggesting the same girlish figure. Here she is on a swing, there she is reading a book while sitting in a deep, low armchair. The notes identify her as 'Lizzie', a young child who was befriended by the artist when he lived in Hampstead. Outraged suspicion about their relationship among local people, the card says, had eventually driven him to reclusion in Oxfordshire.

It's not hard to see why, turning to the adjacent wall, where one finds a much larger landscape canvas showing clearly the same girl yet perhaps ten or twelve years older. Here she lies naked on a single bed, partly covered by a crumpled white sheet, looking straight out at the viewer with wide grey eyes and a self-deprecating smile. Yet this is no classic nude study, for the entire left half of her body and part of her head are translucent and revealing the outline of bone, muscle and tendon as though the artist were, after da Vinci, building up the figure from the inside out but leaving it unfinished. Or perhaps she herself is unfinished. What skin exists is a pale coral whilst the background reverts to patches of abstraction with interwoven primary colours. Within these can be made out, if one is being generous, the shapes of trees, a window with green curtains and a white bridge.

Claire stands before this painting with trembling shoulders and her grip on the wine glass is so light that it is about to fall when a young man in a dark suit, blue shirt and bow tie, appears by her side and takes it from her. He is probably mid-twenties, with an open, handsome face and thick fair hair tied in a ponytail, and he smiles at her sympathetically.

"Some people," he observes softly, nodding towards the brochure in her other hand, "just seem to be born at the wrong time and in the wrong place. Are you feeling all right?"

"I… I think so. Thank you. I just find all this so…"

"Moving?" he suggests. "It's almost unbelievably sad. So much feeling here. But he was always somehow just outside the rest of the world. Never accepted. Or recognised." He gives a small laugh and gestures towards the rest of the gallery where most of the people have their backs to the walls and their attention on one another's forms. "And nothing's changed, eh?"

"He must have been very… alone," she says, more composed now and taking her glass from him. She drinks it down and as though by telepathy the waitress appears nearby offering another. "What's in there?" Claire points towards a small anteroom in one corner, its doorway fringed by long, furled beige curtains.

"Ah," says the young man, "my father wasn't sure – oh, he's the owner of the gallery – whether to include this. It's entirely different. For special clients only. Come and see."

He shows her courteously through to a well-lit space where one wall holds a family of small pieces. They are much later work, landscapes of the Heath, in which the abstraction has all but disappeared. Claire barely glances at them, standing transfixed before the full-length canvas opposite, the figure of an angel in translucent white, fine pale gold stitching at the edges of a low-cut neckline, looking down shyly with a finger to her lips. Behind her the sky is heavy with storm clouds and there are red splashes about her feet that spread along the hem of her gown.

"It's called Clarity," he says. "Some think it represents a presentiment of the artist's death a few weeks later, in a car accident."

"How did it happen?" Claire asks, her voice almost inaudible.

Somehow everything now seems to be further away and going out of focus, as though the walls and ceiling of the gallery are inside out and becoming swallowed in a light mist like the steam of a boiling kettle until they dissolve.

Coming

come
come away
as wooded sunset stalks
this overwhelming night
and calls in all unanswered prayers

come
come away
before the rising wind can sting your eyes
and whip your words away
with fallen autumn smiles

come
come away
and fold that easy face away
the piper pays this tune himself
so come

The Older Woman

masquerading as a waterfall
she flows into a room
inexorable and rushed with gold
while I stand gammy-legged
a white-haired pioneer
panning streams of thought for words
that might just work
with mesh as wide as eyes
and so she slips right through

my outstretched hopes
grip air
and I'm reminded of my youth
and wish that we'd been born
a thousand years ago
and many miles from
age

Enlightenment

Mystery

a mystery
that I should want for you
a freedom
I can never know
for I am bound
entirely
in this love
this boundless
timeless mystery

This Could Be The Last Time

Well, all right, I'll tell you about it. Maybe then I won't have to keep going back after, what, forty years? I know, you're thinking that's stupid, it's crazy to put myself through it even for a week or two every so often. But I have to. Of course, the war did stop me going for a while but then afterwards, even with the place all smashed up like it was, it never really seemed any different. Not to me. I suppose that's because it's all inside.

It's not so unusual to fall in love with Korčula, a lot of people do. It's only small, less than thirty miles long, but it's the most beautiful island, the villages still kept the old culture, and the Adriatic just has that special quality about it around there. It was peaceful too, then, not so many tourists in those days.

For me, though, there was something more, something much deeper, like I actually belonged there and Fate had made a ghastly mistake dropping me in England. Some bozo once tried to tell me

143

it was all to do with past lives, that I was just remembering the place from the eighteenth century or something. And it's true that I seemed to intuitively know my way around and I even picked up the language pretty fast, which is saying something (ever heard Serbo-Croat?). No, that stuff's mumbo jumbo, I just belonged there, that's all. And there was no question in my mind, I was going to stay.

It was easy enough to begin with. My parents had died – there'd been a car crash, no-one ever got to the bottom of it – and I had some money behind me. I got a small, run down house not far from the harbour and started putting it back together. These things aren't so expensive when you know the right people and I was settling in well. Everything seemed second nature to me and the people were friendly. Well, people are when you're in the kaverna most evenings buying them spricers and šljivovica and not asking too many questions.

That's how I got to know Ivan and he asked me to buy into his charter business, in and out of Dubrovnik, mostly taking tourists round the islands. My folks had always done a lot of sailing so I soon picked it up, the local tides, the shady deals and who to trust, that sort of thing. Then Ivan got sick and had to retire so I just took over, along with a good local man to help me. One of the best, Boris Maslovarić. Got himself killed in ninety-four, poor devil. I bet he'd volunteered too, a very straightforward view of life and politics, had Boris. I've always felt I let him down.

I'm just saying. Life was good at the beginning. What's not to like about Dalmatian sunshine, clean air and blue water and good work? Not much spare money, true, but enough to get by and I was where I was meant to be. Okay, maybe I was a bit lonely sometimes – you know how it is, you want to share the good things with someone special, well, share the troubles too. There were one or two local girls, the odd fling with a nice tourist who'd saved up for her two weeks in the sun so she could be not so nice for a while. But nothing that meant anything.

And that's the point, really, because here I was where I was meant to be and all I was waiting for was that someone who… belonged.

I'd be sailing back slowly to the harbour in the evening and imagining her waiting at home for me. She didn't have to be all that beautiful, I had no illusions about myself, but she was kind and gentle and we were made for each other. After a while I could see her clearly in my mind, the Slavic cheekbones, long dark hair and hazel eyes. Ha, even the unshaved legs! I got to looking for her as I walked around the Old Town in Dubrovnik, sure she must be just around the corner one day. I never told anyone else, even Boris. Perhaps if I had he would've put me straight.

So I'd been there about five years when I got the painting. Christ, I didn't even buy it, there was this young street artist I got to know a bit, the hippy sort but a nice guy. Never had two kuna to rub together of course so I used to give him a free ride from time to time over to one of the islands for the day. And one day he just gave me the painting as a sort of payment I suppose. I'd told him I didn't want anything but he insisted that he'd done this one for me and no-one else because I'd been kind to him. It was a weird moment, he said I'd "understand later".

I took a quick look and there she was, my woman with the dark hair and hazel eyes except this girl was younger, maybe mid-twenties. It was a beautiful picture anyway and I was touched. I could feel that strange excitement in my guts, too, you know, like when you know something really important is happening. So I tried to ask Josef – that's the artist – who she was and what he meant about me understanding later, but he was already on the quay and shuffling off. He just called over his shoulder, "Ništa ne mari" – 'It doesn't matter' or something like that. I shouted after him to at least tell me her name because I suppose I thought she must be a real person he knew because the picture was so lifelike. He stopped and turned round for a moment as though he was considering it, but then he shrugged and wandered off and I never saw him again. Later, someone told me he'd gone south.

Yes, I know what you're thinking now, it was just a picture like hundreds of others you see on calendars or advertising hoardings at the side of the road. But this one started burning holes in my head. It haunted me. I hung it over the stone fireplace and stared at it for ages while it stared back at me, and it was only after about a week that I took it down for a closer look and noticed Josef had scribbled something faintly on the back: 'Covek snuje a Bog odredjuje'. You know the saying, 'Man dreams and God decides'. That just made the whole thing even more mysterious. I spent hours looking at it in some kind of trance, convinced that someone was trying to tell me something. But Maria – that's what I called her – looked right back and her lips never moved. Well, of course not, sorry, but I'm telling you that to me she was real. And there was something echoing around inside my head that I couldn't put my finger on.

Do you imagine I didn't also wonder whether I was going mad? Yet I'm telling you that all this, everything that happened, is true. This girl was exactly the one I'd seen clearly in my mind, except younger and with that fresher beauty. And she shattered my contented world within a couple of weeks. I was disturbed, I got anxious, I got impatient with Boris, I took to going off for hours by myself and putting in at some quiet cove to sit thinking about her. I lost customers because I kept forgetting their bookings or I wasn't where I'd said I'd be. In the evenings I stopped going to the kaverna and sat by the fireplace mesmerised by some strange energy that surrounded me, racking my mind for an answer, like… yes, you know when you've had a really powerful dream and you can't quite remember it in the morning but it's still there inside your head, out of reach? Then you spend the next day not properly awake, trying to get it back because you know it wants to tell you something you have to know, and you never can. You never can.

Who was she, what did Josef mean, why was she so important? I wandered around Dubrovnik looking at every face or going to the bars where students and artists hang out, passing round a photo I'd taken of the painting as though she was a missing person. I'm sure they all began to think… well, so did I. I started getting ill, probably not eating properly, definitely not sleeping. At least Boris stood by me, even though he had no idea what it was all about. Like I said, a good man. He tried to persuade me to take a break, go back to England for a while to clear my mind. I knew I could trust him with the business all right, he'd run it better than me lately, but I couldn't leave, I was locked in and anyway England meant nothing to me anymore.

Still, he kept insisting and somehow I knew he was right so eventually I gave in and headed back to Surrey, leaving the painting behind. Maria went with me, all the way, everywhere I went, like she was walking just behind my shoulder or sitting in the next seat. I could almost touch her, she was that close, and I started to feel that, yes, we knew each other. Maybe it was getting away from the island but I did start to relax into it all, into my thoughts about her. She really was my friend, I could feel it. And we were going to be together.

There was a psychic I'd heard about, near Godalming, not my kind of thing but I read that she was well respected by the bozos and the state I was in I'd try anything. I made an appointment, told her nothing and just showed her the photograph. Would you believe, she just shivered slightly and went quiet then eventually said, "This is necessary for you" and "It won't be long" and offered to give me my money back. Well, that just made me even more determined that I wasn't going mad. Probably not what Boris had intended.

Turns out, the weirdo psychic was only right, wasn't she? Boris was away when I got back, visiting his elderly mother, someone told me, so I took the boat out to catch the early evening sun, glad to be back in the warm and the clean air. Back home. I was too tired from travelling to think much about where I was going and after a while I found myself off Hvar to the north so I put in for a break to a small deserted bay I hadn't noticed before, surrounded by woods. I must have dozed off because next thing I knew it was getting late and there was a cool wind getting up. I took a slug from my flask and decided to walk up the hill a bit to get the blood flowing before setting off home.

The woods were more dense and dark than I'd expected and I was just thinking I might be getting a bit lost when I heard the music, just faintly at first, an accordion and some voices laughing and singing. Maybe I could get some food or a hot drink so I headed that way and before long I came out into this clearing. There was a small house on the other side, a whitewashed stone cottage with lamps at the windows and an old wooden door with a crucifix for a knocker. There was a nice stream running past it into the trees and down the hill towards the sea. You'd never see this place from the shore. You'd never know until you were there.

Something about it was making the hairs stand up on the back of my neck. I could still hear the voices and the music but there was no sign of life anywhere about, no-one to be seen through the windows even though I walked all the way round. And I was wide awake by now and still thinking that maybe I could get a drink so I went up to the door. Then it was like someone had turned a switch. Just as I reached for the crucifix, everything went silent and my hand stopped in mid-air like it had a mind of its own. And very slowly, the door opened by itself.

I'm not sure how to say this… Well, very simply, it's just that standing there half in shadow was Maria, or whoever she was. The absolute image, except that this girl in front of me was no more than about seven or eight years old. I tried to speak, introduce myself, but somehow I couldn't, the words wouldn't come, and she just looked me right in the eyes and smiled. Then I thought I could feel someone behind me and turned round but there was no-one there and when I turned back the door was closed and the place was in darkness. I walked all round again but it was deserted. And I just felt cold.

Hell, no, I'm not going to make excuses. That's how it was, that's what happened. I got myself back to Korčula in a kind of daze, my head buzzing. I didn't know what to think but I was, yes, I felt happy, even a bit excited because something was happening and it wasn't all my imagination. Sure, it wasn't what I'd expected or wished for and I didn't understand it. But somehow, on some level, Maria was real. And my life changed again now that I had a clue. Boris came back and was really pleased to see me brighter, anyway, said my holiday had done me good. 'Course, I couldn't tell him about Hvar.

He'd drummed up some new business while I was away so the two of us were at full stretch for a while, no time for brooding or questioning myself. I was enjoying work again and there was good money coming in. Anyway, the strange thing was that the painting didn't have quite same hold over me now. It was still there over the fireplace every evening but it had lost some of its life – or, rather, the life had come out of it and was with me all the time. Do you see what I mean? I don't suppose so. I mean, it was simply a painting now and the feeling I carried around with me was warmer. The girl I'd seen was just a child, I know, yet there was a connection between us now. And I knew there'd be more to come.

After a few weeks there was a bit of a lull in the rush so I took off again on my own for some time on Hvar. You might be wondering why I waited so long. Yes, there'd been work but even so I could have gone. I think it was because somewhere in my mind I knew there was a kind of purpose to it all, destiny or something like that – the psycho had said it was "necessary" – and things would take their natural course. Whatever had to happen was going to happen anyway, so I wasn't impatient. Have you ever felt that, when you know you can sit back until the time is right? It's a great feeling, knowing that everything's in place and you don't have to make things happen.

I put in at Stari Grad, the biggest port, and spent a couple of hours going round the cafés, talking to locals and showing them my crumpled photo. I made up some story about my friend Josef having met this nice girl who'd said her folks had a house up there in the woods but he was too shy, etcetera. I'm sure they saw through it straight away but anyway it was the same thing whoever I asked: there were no houses, no people in those woods to the north. There weren't even any ruddy roads. So late afternoon I put out again and sailed round the headland looking for the bay. I went straight to it, like I was on a string, and in no time I was back in that clearing.

Something was different now and at first I couldn't put my finger on it, even though that other-worldly feeling was back again. Then I realised that although the cottage was there all right, the paintwork was weathered and flaking and the garden neglected. There were no lights and everything was quiet. Then as I got closer I could just make out a couple of low voices, like a mother talking to a child perhaps. This time I held back and waited by the trees at the edge of the clearing, watching the place for any signs of life.

Suddenly the girl appeared, running round from the back of the cottage with a black dog, a Labrador I think, playing and laughing. They stopped a few yards away and looked right at me, the dog growling quietly, and I swear my heart nearly jumped out of my chest. She was just the same, lovely and full of life, except now she was several years older than the last time, almost grown up you might say. Well, it could have been a sister, you're thinking, but I knew it was Maria. It was the same energy.

Emerging

So I said, "Maria?" and she smiled back at me and said, "Dobar dan" then ran back inside. And of course as soon as I took a step forward the switch went off and the place was empty. Was I having some kind of, I don't know, psychotic episode? There had to be something to explain this time slip. Yet I'd never felt better, I was full of life, eating and sleeping well, on top of the work. I felt perfectly sane.

It was getting towards the beginning of September now and business was slowing down so I started visiting Hvar more often. It seemed like the right thing to do, as though things were gathering momentum. Each time, the place looked a bit less cared for and was somehow quieter, if that's possible, like it was slowly dying, while inside me the weird feeling was getting stronger. It was like you get with déjà vu. When things are happening under the surface of your life and are about to break out, you know?

Maria? Yes, I usually saw her there but only ever for a few moments. She could see me too and there was something pulling us together, though she seemed afraid to come any closer. Each time she looked a little older, eighteen, then early twenties. I never saw anyone else although I did hear voices, an older woman who was perhaps her mother, the dog barking, once there was a man shouting in the distance. Boris Maslovarić kept asking me where I was going on my own so eventually I agreed to take him with me. I didn't tell him why I went there, well, I couldn't, could I? I said it was just a nice place I'd found when I was exploring, a peaceful spot. But in my mind I think this was a kind of experiment for me. I might have some confirmation, he'd be a witness so I'd know it was actually real. You can probably guess what happened. I just couldn't find the bay, nothing looked the same, and then a squall blew up out of nowhere and we had to head back.

Whatever it was, I was in this on my own. I had to be alone. Everything about this was, well, a matter of faith. I had to go on with it and keep believing and no-one was going to help me. I had called

Maria into my life by imagining her all those months before. I had seen her clearly in my mind. Precognition, then, or something else? Maybe if I'd been religious I could have, I don't know, prayed or something but there wouldn't have been any kind of answer, would there? I mean, sometimes in life it's just all down to you and what's inside your head and you have to deal with whatever comes.

It got to October and there was a chill in the air, pretty much the end of the season. I used to look forward to this time. A lot of other locals would start feeling low now, not much money coming in with the tourists gone and the Bura winds picking up. The younger ones would all talk about moving away to the cities inland. But I used to love this season, returning to a peaceful life of long breakfasts with štrudla and coffee, fishing by daytime and starting a new book by the fireside in the evening. That was before all this. And this year I had to go to Belgrade for a few days to sort out some papers to do with my residence and the business because the bureaucrats had messed everything up as usual. It took days and days of shuffling around from one office to another, damned annoying, and I hated being away. All the time there was that feeling that things were happening back home and I ought to be there.

When I did eventually get back there was a storm in the air but I put the boat out anyway. I couldn't help myself, I knew that whatever was under the surface was happening right now. And... yes, it was... sorry... this is hard...

Maria was outside, kneeling by the stream and washing her face. It had been really hot, oppressive, despite the season. She was mid-twenties, perhaps, just like the painting now and very lovely. I felt a surge in my heart. I might not have understood what was happening yet here she was, this was it. And she seemed to be expecting me, she watched me as I walked across towards her and this was the first time she hadn't run back to the cottage or disappeared. So for the first time too I could see my imagination realised, her clear skin, soft black hair, a slight smile. Yet I could also sense some sadness in those dark eyes. She stood up and we were no more than a couple of feet apart, the closest we'd ever been, and she must have noticed me shaking with happiness, with relief. I can still feel it now. She was as real as you are.

At last, I thought, I could touch her and I reached out a hand. She lifted hers and for an instant our fingers touched – it was like an electric shock – before she stepped back and looked up at the sky with fear all across her face. My eyes followed hers and I saw the storm approaching, angry and violent. When I turned back she was just gone again. Now I was afraid, terrified to tell the truth, because something almighty was going on.

I barely made it back to Korčula before the heavens fell apart and the lightning crashed as only it can there, a special kind of electrical storm. I was too exhausted to cook anything so I made do with bread and cheese then paced up and down with my šljivovica for… I don't know how long, I must have fallen asleep in the chair because next thing I knew there was this huge crack somewhere to the north at about midnight. I jumped out of the chair wide awake just in time to see the painting fall off the wall into the hearth.

I knew exactly what it meant.

Well, of course it was madness and God only knows how I managed it but I just about got the boat to the north of Hvar on the auxiliary engine. In the moonlight I saw smoke coming up over the trees so I put in and raced up the hill to find the cottage torn apart by flames. I'd never been inside the place before but I wasn't thinking straight anymore so I threw myself at the door, shouting for Maria. It just couldn't happen like this now that I'd found her, now that everything was true, the painting, my dreams, my future.

I found her standing rigid with fear in the back room, clothes and hair on fire, her skin… Christ, it was dreadful, almost more dead than alive. I ripped my jacket off to wrap her and somehow got us both out and into the stream, clinging together tight as chains, our faces pressed close like we were melting with the water rushing over us and stones tearing our flesh. The pain was awful, I remember that. Then nothing else.

I guess it's lucky that Boris was nervous of storms. He went over to my place for company, found the painting burned in the hearth and the boat gone and Heaven only knows how but he put two and two together. A good man. I wish I'd trusted him earlier, told him what was going on. Anyway, he persuaded a couple of the other boats to come after me. They saw my boat and then the smoke over the trees. Huh, lucky? I almost wish they'd never found me, it might have been better.

He said they found me lying burnt up on some rocks at the edge of the clearing. There was a burning tree too, split down the middle by lightning. I'd kept mumbling something about Maria and the cottage but they thought I was delirious. He told me later there was no cottage, there'd been nobody in the area since that last bombing raid, but I made such a nuisance of myself that he and another friend, Željko, took me back there – carried me up the hill – to see for myself. He was right, just a few stones.

I got packed off to hospital and then back to England, because they all thought I'd lost my mind. I couldn't let it go. I wouldn't let her go, she was still there inside my head, clinging onto me, both of us on fire. Nobody has believed me. But I know. I know what really happened.

I have some scars now but everything else is a past life. I go back there from time to time, I have to, and Korčula is still beautiful, so's Hvar, but it doesn't feel the same now that she's gone. I guess Fate dropped me in there and, well, dropped me out again, and I don't know where I belong now.

And every time I go back I tell myself that this could be the last time.

Blood

The airport hangs about us like a bird of prey hovering in the early January gloom, its wings cusped and shadowing its brood of metal chicks scattered patiently on the tarmac. Evening is closing in with cold fingers and the nest is beginning to ice up. Through a misted window I can just make out a huddle of soldiers at the end of a ramp; they're barely out of their mothers' arms but they wear heavy boots, fur caps and greatcoats. And guns. The day's last pale rays of wintry sun trickle over silvered surfaces and back to my blurred eyes. Then it's gone, the window becomes a mirror and all I see are reflections of myself and the guard. Whenever one thinks of this country, one's gaze turns back inward. Many choose not to think.

I turn and a young woman brushes past, a tourist who chose not to think. She has waves of platinum hair and wears a garish red jacket and tight blue jeans tucked into long, brown leather boots, and the mesmerised guard watches her float away. His yellow, grinning teeth are working a piece of gum and his jowls are coarse even though he seems hardly old enough to shave. Why do they give the job of killing to children? The uniform sits on him aimlessly as though still waiting to be put on, yet he's ready enough, a finger playing idly on the holster at his waist. The girl says something to her companions and they look across at us, then turn away and hurry to the souvenir shop while they wait for a tinny voice to tell them they can go home. I have no souvenirs.

He leans over my shoulder and gestures to my writing pad, wanting to know what it is since he can't read English, so I tell him it's a last letter home which seems to satisfy him. No-one must know what I'm going to do or I won't get to finish this for... well, let's just call him John, my travelling companion.

Finally, we're about to fly into an exile that he calls freedom. He's standing there, across the lounge, leafing through some magazines and chatting to his own guard, pink-faced but otherwise a clone of mine. John will find his feet all right and he can hardly wait. Rather grey now, his back less than straight and his lungs weak, he remains irrepressibly alive and bitter. I don't think he's stopped talking since we were released yesterday. His philosophy of life is slightly to the left of a cuckoo's and he asks nothing more of God than a written apology. Well, no doubt he will receive that in Washington.

For the moment, though, he and I are cast out of the role of human being into that of deviant, albeit accidentally. I have no idea what he, a scientist, is supposed to have done or said wrong but I guess he was just careless about choosing the other people in his life. For myself, a journalist can't easily choose anyway but I probably attended too many of the wrong meetings or didn't applaud enough at the right ones. Who knows or cares? I doesn't matter how one breaks the law, only that one breathes it day and night.

My child soldier is clearly getting bored now and a bit careless. He has wandered a few feet away and is frowning over a newspaper pinned to the wall, pretending he can read it and is every bit as good as you or me, but his sullen eyes keep wandering towards a small group of English girls at a nearby table. They're probably students on a politics field trip, with no idea of the earthy politics being played out within a few feet of them. They're laughing about their trip, the awful food, the hotel concierge who carries room keys on a chain like a jailer, and their voices are light and happy. A slender hand runs through soft curls and an unselfconscious leg bare to the thigh rests against a seat. The boy is hypnotised by the flesh. His girl probably has heavy eyes and shoulders and can beat him at cards. His knuckles are white on the holster and it's because of people like him that I weep for this country – not because he's a soldier or a child playing a power game, but because he's slovenly, not doing his job properly, and because he has to have such a girlfriend.

I can make out some of the leading article on the newspaper: 'Our history has been one of consistently consolidating the people's power. The Party will continue to strengthen our society… resolved to defend its gains and protect the people…'

Dear God, what has happened to us? When I was a child, my father read to me every night and I remember being taught at about the age of five that the task of all young people is to master human knowledge and learn the principles of politics by careful study. I was fired with enthusiasm and sense of purpose and I worked at my toys with deter-mination. Then as I grew older I duly studied and mastered. So what went wrong? Somehow I just didn't come to the right conclusions. Perhaps I was just a bad journalist.

Or not moral enough. There's a lot about morals in the stories we tell. Take the one about the hare and the hedgehog having a race (I can't remember why they did and no-one ever seems to have questioned the matter). Being the villain of the piece, the hare was of course both arro-gant and stupid and got talked into a downhill course thinking it would be even easier. But hares can't run downhill and he fell over. Meanwhile, his little brown rival simply curled into a ball and rolled away, onwards and downwards, faster and faster, flying past the winning post unable to stop until he impaled himself on a tree. All the crowd laughed and cheered and then the hedgehog laughed too despite his back being broken and they gave him a medal and a place in history. That's the trouble with most of our stories, the ambiguity of their morals.

I don't think John knows much about morals or is even aware of being taught any. His is a world of predicate calculus, positrons and cloud chambers, and a belief in particles that have to exist whether or not they can be found. He knows every detail about them and has explained their significance to me yet cannot show me one. But I understand that, for don't we all cling to our own elementals? Therein lies our freedom. And there's a lot about freedom – from exploitation, from being used – in our dogma.

On the other hand, I have always remembered some words by an Armenian poet:

> 'At times when my head is cradled
> in the hot palms of your hands,
> at times when my head is laid in
> the scented sweetness of your lap,
> I do not mind, nor call to mind,
> anyone, anything.
> It is simply that my mind is utterly,
> wholly won to the belief
> that, in infinity,
> some planets swirl and whirl as free of our laws of gravity
> as of the grave cares of the world.' [Paruyr Sevak]

Up and down its length and breadth, this airport lounge is so stuffed with people and their parcels that you can hardly tell which is which,

160

all ribboned and tied. Grouped around tables strewn with drinks and magazines, their chatter and animation all enclosed by misted windows, how many, I wonder, consider themselves free? The thought grips my stomach in cold terror.

Only you who have loved another out of sheer necessity, without choice, because your very soul demanded it despite their failings and empty promises, and who have sacrificed yourself to their whim not even willingly but as a matter of spiritual fact, could understand my fear of exile. This is no freedom. It is a banishment from freedom, even though that be a slavery to love. It is banishment to hopelessness and separation. Consider the bride whose groom is killed an hour before their wedding: yes, she may one day find love again but she will never be at peace for as long as she lives. Things must be seen through, whatever the cost.

This country is a lover who is never seen without her make-up. She leaves you standing cold in shops and bus queues, doesn't call when she said she would yet rages at you if you are ever a moment late. She lies beside you whispering softly in the darkness of your night and says she will be yours... soon, but not now. She dances with a light heart when you play the child for her, her laughter warm and comforting and so you only have to follow her and you do. And if things go wrong, how could that ever be her fault? It must be because you have loved her imperfectly, failed to breathe her breath or sigh her sighs, stand between her and her shadows and satisfy her every need before she knows them. This is love. So how could I blame her for sending me away when my life is hers to give and take with a logic all her own?

Of course there are no political prisoners in our country because to suggest that there are is to contravene the criminal code: 'We create conditions favourable for the free and all-round development of the individual...'

I was twenty-nine when I was taken. It was early June and the city streets were filling up, blouses replacing sweaters, hats left at home and the shops packed. Anna and I were buying clothes for our first child, due in three months; we were confident it was a boy so our parcels were full of blue and white. I still remember some tiny socks embroidered with nursery characters and the blue soft elephant with sad eyes that we argued over (I'd wanted the smiling giraffe). Those were the last words we spoke to each other.

We crossed the road by the traffic lights and walked towards the post office because I had to send off a report, and when I swung out of the door again I found myself in the arms of two large men in dark coats who carried me with my own momentum into the back of a black car with its doors open. I opened my mouth to call out but there was no air in me, so I forced my head round towards Anna, a scream on her face, but it was too late. A few people stopped to watch for a moment but then moved on with their lives. All the same, I do think it was unnecessarily public.

It seems that I had circulated malicious and fabricated rumours, abusing my position of respect and responsibility in the community and thus undermining the fabric of our society. There was some more that I forget. Those who oppose the government, as I well knew, may be prosecuted not for their views but for actions that break the law (which has a lot to say about views) and once convicted may be sent for hospital treatment, according to the conclusions of medical experts.

I remember nothing of any experts because I was simply bewildered and hurting, and for some reason I could neither see nor speak very well. The hearing was held – I don't know why – in a cloud. I fell over a few times so clearly I was ill. I had upset my lover, allowed my shadow to overlap hers, and I felt foolish and ashamed, longing to be cured.

Sometime later I was told that Anna had given birth to a boy. He had my eyes and was stillborn. I haven't seen her since that day in June although just once, as I sat alone on a rough wooden bench in the gardens of the clinic, there had been a pale shape beyond the far railings looking in and a feeble beam of esoteric recognition had stumbled across the distance between us. Then as I stooped and strained my eyes towards the shape it had been led away by the trees and I returned to my silence, sitting beside the gravel pathway that only led round in circles and back to some door or other of the clinic. There were no paths to the railings, you'd have to cross the grass and that was forbidden. Where was this clinic? Somewhere outside the city, in the distance.

I had arrived with the early winter, gripped by cold and emptiness, and had to be helped out of the large car with dark windows and up the five or six steps to the heavy wooden doors. Later, from the gardens I would look back and think what an impressive, even beautiful building this was with stone colonnades and carved arches, perhaps the country retreat of a nineteenth century nobleman. Why, then, had he allowed that first room I was taken into to have damp yellow walls, stained linoleum, no window and a single bare lightbulb hanging from brown flex in one corner so that half the room was in shadow as if to disguise the small air vent high up in a corner? And why was the light switch outside?

Several hours or maybe a few minutes later, four men came in wearing white coats, glassy stares and thin smiles that didn't quite reach me. I stood, bent over with one knee shaking, in the middle of the room while they observed me from different angles, consulting their notes and murmuring to one another in soft tones of a language I couldn't understand. I did try to meet the gaze of one, searching his face for some familiar expression, but I couldn't focus properly. I just stood, my soul trembling within paralysed senses.

"Name."

Well, it wasn't a question and even if it had been I couldn't have answered it. I didn't know and I expected them to fall about laughing but they merely jotted and murmured. Gradually, to my surprise I found that I could make out a little of this language, perhaps because I too was desperate to know what was wrong with me so medical terms made more sense than normal sentences.

"Dysarthria."

Hold on, that's not just mental confusion, he's saying I have a cerebral lesion, a material fact. This must be why they gave me that medication before the trial. I wanted to discuss this diagnosis but only managed to raise a hand to my throat and lift an eyebrow and feel stupid, so perhaps he was right.

"Clothes."

Of course I couldn't, the buttons on my shirt were jammed and my shoelaces were double tied so one of them had to do it for me. He was impatient, with cropped fingernails and coarse black hair on the back of his hands. When they brushed my skin they left white marks that I watched dry up and disappear with fascination. I was as curious about my body as they were, probably more so since it seemed to have changed beyond recognition recently, the skin discoloured and flaccid, the shoulders bent inwards, the ribs protruding. They fingered me, inspected me from different positions, lifted my penis then made me lie on my back on that cold linoleum so they could pull each limb and let it fall again. They noted me down then left with my clothes. I tried to cry but even my tears didn't work.

Eventually an orderly came and helped me into a streaked white smock before taking me to a ward where dull eyes watched me from shadowy corners. There was one uncurtained, barred window but no lights. The darkness outside meant that I had been here for hours already. The orderly put me onto a bed with a thin, hollowed mattress and then a doctor came in and injected me. Staring at the ceiling, I'm sure I saw Anna for a moment, smiling down, but then her face swam and disintegrated into coloured globules and I slept peacefully.

'Relaxation of tensions is an important trend... This is a society of genuine freedom. We continue to do everything possible to defend peace...'

This first period of my treatment was shared with five other men, though I can't tell you much about them. I do remember 'Neil', however, a tall and imposing figure whose body seemed to have withstood everything thrown at it. He had deep, restless eyes that watched the rest of us intently from his bed where he'd sit motionless for hours with knees drawn up to his chest. He seemed more aware than the others although I never once heard him speak. But then, few of us did.

For myself, I was in a woolly trance for days, visited every so often by doctors with peering, critical faces but too weak even to turn my head away. Yet very, very gradually I came to feel a kind of gentle and persistent strength within me, a vestige of spirit clinging on by its fingertips, waiting and listening while helpless to play any part in my drama, like a priest hiding behind a secret panel as the enemy search the house. His faint breathing reminded me, at least, of who I was and it was probably his faith that kept me alive.

After a few weeks I would be summoned for regular medical 'consultations'. There were always five doctors present, the four men who had seen me when I arrived together with one woman. She was tall with long black hair tied back, artistic hands and traces of faded beauty in her stern face. These days, a tension had laid siege to the corners of her eyes and lips and thin lines had begun to etch her skin. Care had lost ground in the pale green eyes though it was still there somewhere for it was always she who tempered the harsher, dismissive judgements of the men as they discussed me. There was no attempt to hide this from me; I would just be standing there limply, no more than an object of curiosity as though I were a chair with a broken leg placed before a committee of carpenters.

As I grew a little more sensible, it was to Olga – I gave them all names since none were volunteered – that I looked with a glimmer of hope for the future. She was clearly a psychologist so surely she would understand. Yet of course she was in fact the cruellest of them all, the one who degraded me the most and tore down whatever bridge I tried to build between us. It was Olga who would, without warning, ceremony or apparent reason, order me to strip naked and then cover every part of me with a cold, empty stare until I wanted to weep for forgiveness. It was Olga who would order one or other of us to be taken to the yellow room, to be beaten for some offence we didn't know existed and left there for maybe three days, and who would come later with a bowl of slop and slide it across the floor to us so that there was almost nothing left. And I would silently wipe away the food and return her pitying look, convinced that all this was necessary and for my own good.

She never came into the ward – that would have been too dangerous – but if she walked into this airport lounge now I would kneel and offer my hand.

The consultations, the inspections, the beatings were regular. The meals of boiled cabbage or fish were regular. We got up with the dawn and went to bed with the sunset. The ward was a regular hexagon.

We did nothing for ourselves. There was neither work nor exercise. There were no books, just a radio with its controls out of our reach. Meals were brought and taken away, drugs were taken meekly. Our clothes didn't fit us. The only way to survive was to accept the routine, to welcome uniformity and tell oneself that this was no constraint but indeed an expansion of the self. After all, the helpless watching priest would say, is it not the Word of God to abandon one's life for the greater freedom of union with the Almighty?

'The personality has the highest value in our culture. However, it can develop fully only in a harmonious society of equals... The stability of the community depends on a solidarity of interests.'

I can't say what happened to my personality and, as I've said, for a while I even forgot my name. But they had to call me something so I learned it again. At least, I assume it's my name although since I didn't choose my original name anyway it probably doesn't matter. Along with the other men in the ward, I soon lost interest in the reasons for our being there. And I got headaches when I thought about Anna, so I stopped. Personality? That was quite irrelevant compared to the fascination we developed for our own bodies, the changing colour of skin, the growth of fingernails, the quality of excrement and the rise in temperature after the sulphur injections. That fire would race through the arteries, burning them up like a jet on take-off and lifting us out of our lethargy into endlessly shifting positions, kick-starting our voices into hollow rage until the new fascination with the sweat pouring off us in storms took over. I have no idea what the reason was for this. But then, if your doctor gives you an aspirin do you demand a detailed explanation with diagrams and equations? Anyway, I used to smoke a packet of cigarettes a day before all this but I can't touch them now because of the fire you have to use to light them, so I'm better off for it.

Later, I would involuntarily vomit at the merest memory of those days. It was Olga, who had derided and degraded me, who had watched me disintegrate and to whom there was no part of me that hadn't been exposed, who slowly put me back together with kind words of understanding. It wasn't that she helped me forget. On the contrary, she would remind me constantly of my human impotence and helped me to see that this is the way of all life.

And so I came to see that my lover was not punishing me at all but rather, with limitless love and painstaking care, was saving me from the hell into whose depths I had fallen. That was Neil's mistake, you see, to refuse this love. I had at first thought that his totally silent resistance to everything was a show of consummate inner strength, that his lack of any outward reaction even to the sulphur exemplified superhuman self-control, a great virtue. But one day it killed him, so what had he achieved? There is no strength in clinging to self.

There's a fog coming in now, inexorably swirling and blurring the faint tail-lights outside. Some of the ground crew have retreated up inside the boarding ramp as far as the swing doors at the other end of the lounge to catch some warmth. One chats to the girl on duty by the metal detector and her light laugh at something he's said travels faintly across to me. This place is getting more and more crowded now as flights are delayed and the boy is scowling at a group of large Swedish men who are chatting to the English girls and blocking his view.

John is getting annoyed with all the waiting and is staring angrily out of the window as if to challenge the fog. But it makes no sense to be frustrated with climate, even when it stops you doing what you want to do (or, in this case, get on with the rest of your life). It's the rhythmic breathing of our world and far greater than us, and we must live and breathe with it. Our lives change with the same persistent patterns. From the humblest man to the greatest state, we rise and fall, thoughts flowering and expectations soaring before dark nights suppress them and lead to all but lifeless days when there is nothing to be done but draw up the blankets around our hope and wait for a new season. Even so, there is no absolute guarantee the sun will rise tomorrow, no sworn affidavit that winter cannot follow winter. And if it did, who are we to complain? Our lives are rooted in probability and belief, and acceptance that both may be wrong is surely the greatest wisdom.

Yet it was indeed spring when I finally left the ward to begin what they called my convalescence. I saw flowers for the first time in… what, two years? I saw a pale smudge against the railings. And for the first time I saw from the outside the place that had been my home. There was ivy on the stone walls, starkly outlined against the cool blue of an April sky, and it looked to me like one of the mansions of Heaven especially as it was set amongst all those paths that went nowhere except back to itself.

In the same grounds but perhaps half a kilometre away and separated by a tall barbed wire fence was, as I would later discover, the even more imposing teaching hospital, a monument to the god Medicine that swallowed up and poured forth dozens of people daily. At lunchtime the surrounding gardens would overflow with white-coated young men and women strolling in groups or sitting in pairs, presumably debating the finer points of cases or playing the tactical word games that people do when they want something.

I watched from the other side of the fence and a hundred years away, silent and alone. Even the birds preferred the other side since I had no crumbs for them. Sometimes there would be a few of us dotted about the winding pathways, incongruous lumps huddled on our rotting benches, barely enough of us to hang our oddments of new clothing on. I had been given a rough grey shirt and vast shapeless trousers tied at the waist with string, which must have been made for a giant lumberjack so long were they that they dragged about my feet leaving trails of dust. The quiet was broken only by the faint hum of life beyond the fence or a coughing fit as 'Thomas' drew on his handrolled cigarette and hacked the air for a minute. Thomas had TB and perhaps three months to live, so there was no point in trying to get him to give up.

Occasionally a couple of us would be allowed to sit together but even so we wouldn't speak for maybe half an hour or more, then exchange half a dozen words before lapsing back within ourselves. I tried to think but it was a slow and painful process, body aching and head swimming with nausea, but it felt like I had to do it to reassure myself that my brain hadn't dissolved. You hadn't been able to think in the early days because of the electrical treatment: they put the electrodes laterally across your head when they wanted to 'calm' you. The anaesthetic usually didn't work so you'd writhe under the straps like an epileptic thinking your back was breaking, but when it was over you'd come out of it with a dullness between your ears and your problems wouldn't seem so great.

During the long, warm months of that summer I slowly gathered strength. I also got friendly with John. Well, it wasn't exactly the sort of friendship you might have with a workmate, jokes about the boss and discussing last night's football and the like. Rather it consisted of sharing the same bench. But in a clinic you get very jealous of private space so to share it when you don't have to is real friendship, and the closeness of another human being, albeit a broken down one, is enough. Sometimes in the late afternoon I would watch the dutiful visiting relatives trooping into the hospital across the fence and imagine them sitting awkwardly in the wards, trying to think of things to say. If only they realised that you do much more good by sharing a cup of tea, being nearby for a few minutes and keeping your mouth shut. Much later, John and I would have a faltering game of chess together and get talking to each other, he of his particles and I my travels, and pretty soon we knew each other less.

In springtime, the vibrant life of the flowerbeds was almost intimidating. But by late summer we'd overcome this and might hazard a slow, circuitous tour of the gravel pathways, in and out of azaleas and yellow roses to the bench nearest the tall wire fence. From there we'd imagine that we could make out some of the distant figures, especially the young women, nurses and visitors, white uniformed and floral skirted. They became our preoccupation as we tried to remember what it was like to touch a woman…

'…cradled in the hot palms of your hands…
my head laid in the scented sweetness of your lap…'

Once we had relearned the basics of conversation, we would invent scenarios and imagine ourselves casually walking alongside one or other pretty nurse, teasing her and getting closer. Of course it was stupid, we knew perfectly well what we looked like, what we would be to them, but I suppose it was a kind of new adolescence, like shy seventh graders fantasising over the high school goddess. And if we were ever in danger of forgetting ourselves, there was always Olga to remind us.

"Strip."

It didn't matter the time of day or place, in ward or corridor, she could make us submit in the cause of our recovery to another cold inspection, another reminder of our foolishness and another couple of days in the yellow room, as though she really could read those lascivious boyish thoughts. Indeed, could I really imagine this skinny, yellowed body lying alongside the pretty nurse with the soft hair and perfect small breasts? Even if an unexpected thought of Anna appeared, the whole idea soon filled me with fear and I put her out of mind again. What do you say when you meet an old lover in the street after half a lifetime?

"I did once know a girl," John told me falteringly one day, with long pauses of effort, as we sat staring at the fence. "Everyone thought we'd get married… I think I probably did love her… Do you know what stopped me?" I shook my head obligingly. "Presents… that was it, Christmas and birthday presents… She always bought people things that she liked… never a thought for whether they'd like it… as though their beauty would be self-evident to anyone… So that made me think…" His voice trailed off, following his eyes into the past.

Yet strangely, I knew exactly what he meant because it's what every man fears, that his girl is only with him for appearances' sake or for what she can get out of your relationship. Do women love like men do?

"Do you think I was right?" he asked, and I almost laughed aloud at the irony of it, considering who and where we were now, longing for a girl's merest touch.

"How can anyone answer that?" I said instead with a shrug. "If you loved her, perhaps it wouldn't have mattered. Who knows? Everyone has to make… sacrifices. Did you choose her so you could make a present of her to someone else?"

Somehow this seemed a logical point at the time and he reflected on it for ages, far longer than it deserved, before finally putting his head in his hands and mumbling, "I should have married her, then."

It was Olga who told me that I was going to be released. Or rather, exiled. She spat it at me. I suppose she thought her work had been wasted. In any case, I never saw her again and none of the other doctors ever spoke another word to me even during my last inspection, the passing out parade of pale, worn flesh.

We found out what had happened from a sympathetic orderly who'd overheard an enraged conversation between Olga and a visiting politician. An American journalist investigating the psychiatric clinic had slipped through security by posing as a hospital visitor on the other side of the fence (there had even been a real patient inside for him). Somehow he'd managed to take a few photographs across the gardens and there were John and me on our bench girl-watching. By some unworldly fluke, one of his colleagues recognised us and protests were raised, the spirit of international treaties broken, that sort of thing. So they couldn't keep us then and we were being tossed out, like half-eaten prey given up by a wild dog to a vulture, with a growl.

It took quite a while to sink in. We were isolated from the others, given good regular food and daily physiotherapy, and measured up for decent clothes. Confined together now, John and I got to exchanging plans and regrets in equal measure. He was the more joyful, with little to leave behind, and even if the other world's welcome should cool in time it was still for him a place of opportunity. I was more troubled. After the first rush of anticipation I found myself asking the same question over and over again: was it all for nothing that I had spent these last years in the wilderness? And then there was a second question: what would have happened had the American not chanced upon us? Surely my lover, having taken such care, would not then have rejected me...

On my last night at the clinic I had a dream that woke me, soaked in sweat, at three in the morning, the Hour of the Wolf. I was travelling across this country yet managed to arrive (as dreams have it) in Rome, where I was taken prisoner by a huge, masked figure. It had the body of a woman, but coarse and muscled, and a blinding white light shone from eye slits in the mask. She whipped me and left me for dead, hanging on a tree. But my bonds dissolved and I hurried away in the black of night on a road signposted to the docks, arriving at sunrise to see a great ship hovering there like a phoenix. A group of sailors up on deck urged me aboard and threw a rope ladder over the side, but my bruised hands were fumbling with identity papers and my swollen feet could barely move. When I looked up, the ship was just a pale smudge against the horizon. Then it started snowing and, as I bent my head, drops of blood fell silently from my eyes to the pure white ground.

I am not leaving on this aeroplane. In a few minutes, while the boy is distracted, I'll slip these papers into John's overcoat pocket with a wink. He's a good man at heart and knowing how much we've shared he won't question me. Then of course, when they ask what I've been writing, I'll take out the other letter that I wrote yesterday. It denounces your world and all your values as hypocrisy, your materialistic society as cruel and uncaring. It swears my love for my country and promises to undertake whatever work is required of me. It asks only that I might return to Anna, who will believe that it was all for her sake. Maybe, in time, we'll be able to have another child.

You probably think that I am, as Solzhenitsyn had it, an ant returning to its burning log in the bonfire from sheer instinct. Actually, I don't care in the least what you think. I am a lover and a believer and neither you nor any of your superficial gods can change that.

Alongside the principles of politics, I once learned another poem that has somehow stayed with me, if not its precise words then at least in spirit:

> 'I solemnly declare that I have lived no worthless year
> nor trodden any road without reason
> nor do I regret my love,
> though I be deceived and wounded,
> whose pure light is in me still.
> It will never be too late to start afresh
> and, from the past, I shall wipe out
> no single word.'
> (Olga Bergholz, *A Wayfarer's Letters,* 1962)

The First Wish

How do you feel about canals? Personally, I've never been that impressed. Yes, I know they're our heritage and the Stoke potters needed to get their stuff down to the Severn and on to Bristol. But I don't imagine anyone would be that keen on the one at the back of our estate. The Smestow branch of the Staffs and Worcs is in a class of its own, a long and limp, sickly pea-green stretch of water that any prophet could easily walk across on account of all the shopping trolleys and pieces of garden shed lurking just below the surface. Where other rural waterways amble peacefully, the Smestow drags itself painfully, teeming with noxious microbiology, through the least interesting bits of Staffordshire.

So you'd be justified in wondering why, on this particular Sunday afternoon, I was happily meandering alongside this stretch of historic England. The reason was, simply, Gaynor. More specifically, that Gaynor was wearing a light cotton summer dress at least two sizes too small for her. This was not normal for her, being what she called a practising Catholic with very strong views, often solemnly expressed to me, about unseemly behaviour inciting the baser instincts of youth. We are talking mid-Sixties. These must have been challenging beliefs for a nineteen year-old girl of her breathtaking stature, with eternal slim legs and cascading blonde hair that surely caused many a bout between priest and conscience. Satan himself would have had difficulty getting himself behind her.

I confess to having been in love (if that's the right word) with Gaynor since sharing the same class at Warstones Junior School. She was already beautiful at the age of ten. She knew it too and kept herself coolly aloof from all the boys' pathetic prepubescent advances. It still hurts to remember the time I passed her a small, thoughtful gift under cover of our adjacent wooden desks only to see it immediately dropped to the floor and crushed underfoot. At Break our class teacher, Mrs Wallace, had called me back after the others left, fixed me with a smile that was at once kindly and withering, and said, "She's out of your league, son."

So she was. Despite her living at the farmhouse just down the road, our paths rarely crossed during the turbulent teenage years, though her image lingered unforgotten in a locked dark room at the back of my mind. Yet, as the gurus always say, things change… (Of course, there weren't any gurus at those pre-Maharishi times and it's only in the modern day, now that a plethora of them have descended from the Himalayas with their other-worldly messages, that I can tell this story without fear of ridicule. It's true, honest.)

It was high summer and I was home from university after a first year of exposure to the outside world, so naturally I needed to get away from the house, whose other occupants were still far from embracing the outside world, as much as possible. On its creation, our estate had been absentmindedly left just outside the nearest town so I was in the habit, when there were lawns to be mowed or washing up to be done, of wandering the nearby countryside composing the next hit single in my head. A short distance along the main road, a narrow rutted lane led past the farm before narrowing to nothing and losing itself in open fields (something of a metaphor for Staffordshire itself).

Gaynor bounced across the cobbled courtyard as I approached and leaned precipitously over the sagging five-bar gate. Whether she'd been absolved at church that morning or just hadn't been practising hard enough lately, she seemed to be in a strangely free-thinking mood, as was her dress which was making no real effort to do its basic job.

"Nice out, isn't it?" she called gaily and perhaps unnecessarily. I paused, dumbstruck at the sight of her and especially by a welcoming smile I would have killed for a decade earlier. "My folks have gone off visiting, left me all alone."

"Oh?" The inflection of my voice and eyebrows would have been obvious to a monk.

"I'm bored. We could go for a walk round the farm if you like."

"Oh." There was a marginal droop of features.

"Or we could go down by the canal. I do love canals, don't you?"

"Oh."

My vocabulary might not have been at its most impressive at this point but it had a remarkable flexibility of tone. I managed to stammer something about how lovely that would be and so it was that some twenty minutes later I found myself picking my way gingerly beside the crawling nether regions of the Smestow branch in the wake of a continuous prattle about the magnificent Shire tow horses that had long since preceded us, although not that long since judging by the state of my shoes.

This flaccid stretch of water was being considerably enhanced by Gaynor and my feelings towards canals were becoming less hostile. If truth be told, they were being almost completely overridden by certain other feelings as a key turned in the lock of a dark room at the back of my mind. We reached a wide open expanse of common land covered in long grasses and wild flowers. It was a warm sunny day. As far as the eye could see, Staffordshire was deserted except for me and a very beautiful, very friendly young woman in a very short dress. I shall leave those other feelings to your imagination.

Gaynor really was in a strange mood. She let me catch up and then walked alongside me, linking her arm in mine, and began chatting away about how glad she was to be living on a farm because she loved nature so much although her mind often struggled to reconcile pantheism with her faith and did I think she would ever resolve the issue? Personally, I had little doubt about the present state of the battle. Furthermore, when the farmhouse behind us had dropped below the horizon and she suggested we might rest for a while in a large grassy hollow, you could definitely hear mournful celestial trumpets blowing the retreat.

I hardly knew what to think by now, in fact thought was almost certainly the last thing on my mind. The Angel of Class 4A was here beside me and within reach after all this time. Praise the gurus. It hadn't been an easy adolescence, to be honest, and I'd never had much self-confidence. There'd been that crushing rejection at the age of ten, far too much schoolwork and far too little proper education, the local soccer team was sliding down the leagues and my parents had threatened total disinheritance if I ever bought a Rolling Stones record. So I was now working on pure human instinct.

Gaynor began slowly and elegantly to lean backwards invitingly, 'to make herself more comfortable', and the dress took another three or four inches northwards. It was when I thought I ought to say something nice that events – and to this day I can hardly believe this really happened – took a sudden and surprising turn.

"You know, Gaynor, I've always—"

"Stone me, this ent gettin' babby a pinny."

We both hung in mid-teeter like half-deflated balloons with disproportioned smiles frozen on our faces, looking at each other with wide, staring eyes.

"You never moved your lips," I whispered hoarsely after a moment.

"Nor did you." Then it came again, thin and high-pitched but perfectly clear.

"They'm never gerrin' it done in a rain o' pigs' pudding."

We eased ourselves slowly back upright with foolish expressions locked on our faces like children caught with an empty biscuit tin and peered cautiously over the lip of the hollow. Nothing. There was no getting away from the fact that as far as the eye could see in every direction there wasn't the slightest sign of intelligent life except for a handful of sheep several hundred yards away. We mutually agreed in trembling whispers that it was probably asking too much of a sheep to have picked up Black Country dialect even in a lifetime of standing in a field with nothing else to do. With my new-found knowledge of university student social behaviour, I wondered briefly whether perhaps some rare fumes had undetectably crept over us from the canal and taken hold of our reason. But no, it was the wrong sort of weed.

When we heard the voice again, making an impolite comment about the parentage of undines and sylphs, there was no doubt where it was coming from however much we didn't want to believe it. Sitting cross-legged on the ground between us, hidden in the grasses and leaning back comfortably against Gaynor's calf, was a figure about nine inches tall wearing a green jerkin and dirty yellow trousers. He was muttering to himself and shaking his head, causing fine wisps of long white hair to toss from side to side.

We stared at him for a moment, then at each other, then back at him. This performance went on for a full minute until Gaynor let out a strangled shriek and pulled her knees up to her chin. The poor chap had no chance at all and went right over onto his back with legs and arms flailing before picking himself up and scuttling behind a clump of taller grasses. Presently a little head peeped out from the stalks and observed us warily.

"Well, I'll goo to the foot of our stairs," he squeaked nervously. "Yo day 'arf gi'us a turn then. Us never thought as 'ow yo could 'ear us." His eyes narrowed as he observed us closely. "Yo's not s'posed to, y'know. 'Appen your minds was very much on nature jus' then, eh?" This much was true at least. I went through all the usual physical actions of replying but for some reason no sound was coming out of me and it was Gaynor who recovered first.

"Well, sort of... yes, but... then we never thought... I mean, we didn't..."

"Aye, us knows what yo mean, wench," the little chap interrupted. "Them as believes in us is 'arf soaked, ennit? Any road up, yo do an' that's summat. An' yo's the fust to see us sin' that farmer shot us hat off thinkin' us were a rabbit two year back. Barmy, eh? What's a rabbit doin' in yellow briches?" He had clearly decided that we were harmless and now reappeared from behind the grasses offering a tiny hand to each of us in turn. We numbly extended little fingers. "Well, well, visitors. This am bostin'. I'm, er, Pan."

"What, you mean... *the* Pan?" asked Gaynor. She was adjusting to the situation rather better than me. "You haven't got any pipes." The fellow looked down at his feet and shuffled a bit.

"Um, no. They'm very 'ard to play, y'know." There was a long pause while he considered our new relationship carefully. "Orlright, if yo mus' know Pan's jus' a sort o' nickname. It gets lonely 'ere wi' no-one to talk to 'cept the devas – 'oo do' answer back – an' life 'as to 'ave a bit o' romance." He sat down again, leaning back against Gaynor's leg since she was clearly his favourite for some reason, and looked a bit sad. "Us common elves do' 'ave names."

"Aaaah," Gaynor said sympathetically. "Never mind. Tell you what, we'll give you a name if you like. We'll call you—" she looked around desperately for an appropriate clue and saw only daisies and dandelions "—um, how about Dandy?" It was the better choice. Maybe it wasn't a masterpiece of creative imagination but the elf definitely perked up at the thought of having his very own name.

"Who are the devas?" I asked, feeling it was time I made a contribution to the conversation. I looked around cautiously, half expecting us to be ringed by small green figures heavily armed with sharp sticks.

"Oh, do' fuss yo'sen, ower kid, yo' wo' see 'em. No'un sees 'em 'cept me. They'm jus' innergy, they do' 'ave proper bods an' that. But," he puffed himself up proudly, "us controls 'em an' we grow the flowers an' that." He spread out an arm to indicate the fields around us and prove how busy he'd been lately.

You will appreciate that all this was quite a lot to take in. I was beginning to collect my thoughts by now – the few that hadn't already been scattered out of my brain to the four winds – and tell myself that a year of higher intellectual learning at one of England's finest institutions didn't sit well with the concept of supernatural beings, in yellow trousers or otherwise. I mean, I'd never even been the least bit superstitious. Not like my mate Dave. Dave would fall over every time he stood up because he'd forget to uncross his legs. And he was always late for football because he refused to get on a number thirteen bus. Dave would have had no trouble at all accepting the reality of imaginary and shapeless invisible forces. Dandy could somehow read my mind…

"Yo do' believe us, do' yo?"

"'Course we do," Gaynor said quickly, reaching forward to pat his tufty head whilst shooting me a meaningful dark look. Some people, I thought, will believe anything. But then, if I was to make any progress with Gaynor and, as it were, pick up where we, as it were, left off,

I was clearly going to have to give my attitudes a good talking to. I tried again.

"So why yo gorra cob on when we met yo, Dandy? Yo' 'ad a face like Livery Street." A bit of dialect might just endear me to him. It didn't. He just squinted suspiciously at me from the corner of one eye for a full minute before the need to chat overrode mistrust.

"Yo sin the state o' the cut?" He gestured over our shoulders towards the turgid, murky waters of the Smestow.

This turned out to be his favourite subject for today and there followed a long, rambling diatribe about the state of nature in these parts and how the undines had all but given up on the canal as a thankless job and how devas were being laid off left, right and centre and how there was no incentive anymore to grow wild flowers out in the middle of nowhere next to smelly waterways because you're just not appreciated, oh no you're not, and how in any case if anyone did happen to pass this way and notice his flowers they just picked them so he had to start all over again and how most of the other local elves had put in for transfers so he was practically the last one left with no-one to talk to.

"Never mind, eh," Gaynor put in when he paused to draw breath. "We love your flowers and promise not to pick any. Don't we?" She shot me another of those glances. I nodded willingly, picking flowers having been the last thing on my mind for a while. "What's more," she went on, "we'll tell all our friends to come and visit you. How's that?" I wasn't at all sure how that conversation was going to go but the idea certainly appealed to Dandy, whose tiny eyes lit up like fireflies.

"That's bostin', ta very much. Let's drink on it."

He jumped nimbly to his feet and scurried off, returning soon after with a large buttercup under each arm – no, the moral inconsistency of this was not lost on me but I suppose it all depends on one's motives – which he filled with some difficulty with minute drops of crystal clear dew from the grasses before proffering them to us.

"This am nice!" He beamed with the pleasure of new-found friendship while we sipped our dew as slowly as possible (which I can tell you is not easy when you're drinking out of a buttercup). As we racked our brains for something to say, this not being a normal Sunday afternoon conversation, Dandy also seemed to withdraw in thought until suddenly he had an idea and jumped around the hollow excitedly.

And this is where the day took a strange turn.

"I gorrit, ower kids. Sin yo've bin so nice an' cheered us up no end, us wants to do summat for yo. So us'll grant yo two wishes. There!"

"Beg pardon?" I nearly choked on my dew.

"Us says, I gorrit, ower kids. Sin yo—"

"Yes, we got that, Dandy. Um, are you sure you can do that?"

"Yo mean, us bin just an elf an' that?" He was clearly affronted and giving me that squint-eyed look again. "Yo knows nuthin' 'bout nature, yo saft beggar."

Suitably chastised, I murmured an apology and glanced across at Gaynor who hadn't said a word recently. She too was struck rigid, except for a secret-feminine-pleasure kind of smile laying siege to the corners of her mouth as she considered the unimaginable possibilities.

"Wishes!" she breathed eventually. "For us. Anything we want."

"Ar, within reason," said Dandy, drumming his fingers on my foot impatiently waiting for a decision. And reason is where the whole thing began to unravel.

"Just think," Gaynor turned to me, "of all the things we could have."

"Two things," I reminded her. "And if we're to take this situation seriously we need to do some pretty careful thinking first." Perhaps unfortunately, my year of higher intellectual learning was now beginning to intrude on my brain. Let's be honest, personally I'd pretty much had only one wish on my mind ever since an hour or so ago when I'd seen Gaynor bouncing across the farm courtyard, but I couldn't very well ask any sort of fairy for that. Instead, I forced myself toward deeper philosophical considerations.

"Hmm... world peace... justice... spiritual enlightenment..." I mused.

"Fur coat... Aston Martin DB5... Omar Sharif..." breathed Gaynor, in the philosophical shallows for the moment. It's a curious phenomenon that when it comes down to a shoot-out, so to speak, many self-professed religious people tend to lose sight of more aesthetic ideals. Or perhaps, as I observed earlier, she had just been absolved and was free to work on a new confession.

"Now just a minute," I objected, turning to her seriously and fighting off the melting sensation throughout my body, "this is quite a responsibility, you know. I mean, this doesn't happen every day. We could have the entire future of human civilisation in our hands at this moment. One slip of the tongue and everything could be wiped out, canals, wild flowers and all."

"Not sure us could stretch to that," remarked Dandy drily, "but yo's right to think on. Do' make it too 'ard, eh? Us am a bit out o' practice."

"Right... then..." I said slowly so that my brain could catch up. "We clearly have an ethical obligation to accentuate the theoretical potential altruistically for the ultimate and permanent benefit of—"

"You what?" said Gaynor, screwing her face up.

"Saft beggar," said Dandy.

"So for our first wish," I continued undeterred, "I would like – as many wishes as we want. There." I leaned back in the grass and beamed triumphantly. To give Dandy his due he recovered quite fast, having first fallen onto his back with a moan and then done a couple of somersaults on my chest before giving my nose a good tweak and settling himself back down against Gaynor's leg.

"Yo's 'aving a loff, ower kid. Nahhh, us did say 'within reason'. An' if yo think on't what yo' jus said ent logcly valid sin the offer were fer two wishes. Nice try, though." If I'd been wearing a hat I'd have taken it off to him; he might have been small but he certainly wasn't stupid. Gaynor had been very quiet during this metaphysical exchange and now felt it was her turn.

"You know," she began, frowning slightly, "I've been wondering. It's a funny thing but when I really think about the possibilities and all the things I could have and, I mean, examine my inner motives, like…" She paused. It was quite an impressive build-up but the sequel was delivered almost apologetically. "…then there isn't anything I really want for myself. I'm quite fond of the old car Dad got me even if it does rattle a bit and I've got plenty of nice clothes…" Possibly not the right size, though, I wondered. "…and I bet even Omar Sharif isn't that great when you get to know him. Probably snores.

"And what's more," she went on, addressing me directly, "have you thought what you'd say to everyone if you suddenly walked in one day with a yacht under your arm – and what would happen next? This place would get trampled down by hordes of people demanding wishes off of Dandy and picking his flowers." My heart followed the rest of my body in warming to her.

"You're probably right," I agreed. "So we have a momentous decision before us. We need to consider the state of international relations—"

"The balance of societal power—"

"The hidden forces of reaction—"

"And the indigenous cultural heritage—"

"Yes, the struggle of the proletariat—"

"The inequality of natural resources—"

"Leading to exploitation of the under-privileged—"

"And of animals—"

"Indeed, the spirit of nature—"

"The effect on ecumenical tolerance—"

"And individual freedom of expression—"

"Not to mention the development of personal consciousness—"

"And what about the subatomic structure of matter—"

"And relativity—"

"Then there's the cosmic perspective—"

"Yes, there is that."

Dandy had been watching us throughout this exchange like a tennis umpire, his little ears spinning from one side to the other and back again until he got dizzy and fell over again. I helped him up while he scratched his head and sighed.

"I dunno," he muttered, "yo two gorra right bob on. It were never like this in the noggy days. An 'andsome prince or a big bag o' ackers an' it were all over in a minute."

"Ah, well maybe so," I countered, "but that was before Descartes, Engels and Wittgenstein, wasn't it?"

"'Ooever they are—"

"And another thing," Gaynor interrupted, her eyes narrowing and an expression of what looked uncomfortably like piety gathering on her brow, "I'm sorry, Dandy, but how do we know we can trust you? I mean, Father Gabriel was saying only this morning that we must be on our guard against the Devil who will promise us all manner of worldly things but what shall it profit a man, and I'm pretty sure that includes women, if he—"

"Charmin'!" Dandy did a passable impression of an explosion.

"Yes, steady on," I agreed. "I know I was a bit sceptical at first but that's going too far." I was personally fairly confident that if the Devil were around and in tempting mood he wouldn't have been so thoughtless as to interrupt the activities of an hour or so ago just as they were getting darkly interesting by taking the innocuous form of an nine-inch elf.

"Thank yo, ower kid. Divil indeed." Dandy bowed courteously to me and strolled around a bit to calm down before hauling himself up onto my knee to demonstrate where his favour currently lay. "Us 'as never bin so insulted. An' us 'as only tryin' to help yo." He paused to reflect for a moment before turning the argument on Gaynor. "Anyroadup, if that's what yo think us is, then jus' wish us day exist an' then yo's all saved." There was a definite touch of bitterness in his voice.

"Ah, sorry," I felt I had to steady the philosophical ship, "no offence or anything but I don't think that quite follows. See, for one thing if you didn't exist – whoever you are – then neither would this situation which includes Gaynor and me. And we can hardly wish ourselves out of existence, can we? The premise is polemically unacceptable." He cocked his head on one side.

"Hmmm, us sees what yo's gerrin' at. Do go on."

"And for another thing," I looked across at Gaynor with an apologetic shrug, "if we follow through on the rational parameters of the matter, I don't think we can ask anything for other people after all. Take world peace, for example. It could only be created in our own personal perspective, so we might believe it but would anybody else? This is endemic to the whole dilemma. Anything we wish for could only be true for us, so it would have to be essentially selfish after all."

There was a very long, uncomfortable silence while Gaynor gazed wistfully at her conscience and Dandy did a lot of head scratching, perhaps regretting waking up today, and I began to wonder whether mowing the lawn might not have been such a bad option.

"Right," said Dandy decisively at last, "there's only one way to sort this clartin' about. We'm gooin' to see Mother."

Without more ado and clearly not in the mood for any argument, he carefully selected a long, sharp blade of grass, stood very still in the middle of the hollow mouthing something under his breath, then held the blade at arm's length and very carefully cut a tear in the fabric of the universe before pulling it open and gesturing Gaynor to come through after him.

"C'mon, bab, gi'us yer donnie. Then yo." He looked back over his shoulder at me and I meekly took Gaynor's other hand as we stepped, without complaint, out of our world.

It's odd what you can do when you put your mind to it.

We found ourselves in an earthen tunnel that somehow seemed to adjust itself to our height, illuminated by tiny crystals in its walls and ceiling and clearly well-trodden. Dandy trotted on ahead, chattering all the while about how this was a great honour and we could do much for The Cause, whatever that was.

"Slow down a bit," I called to him, stopping to catch my breath. "Exactly why are we going to see your mother?" He turned and fixed me with a kindly and withering look that Mrs Wallace would have been proud of.

"Not my mother, yer daft aypeth," he said, "Mother Earth."

"Ah, I see."[1]

"Of course," echoed Gaynor, with a mystified look towards me. But by now we may as well just accept whatever happened. We plodded along for what seemed ages until suddenly our path was blocked by a creature twice as tall as Dandy and definitely more menacing. He was quite amazingly ugly with brooding piglet eyes above a long, horribly crooked nose

---

[1]   In case you're wondering, I did later ask Dandy why, of all the beautiful and majestic places she could have chosen, Mother Earth had installed herself in this unprepossessing area of Staffordshire. He gave me another of those looks and several unrepeatable insults before pointing out with welcome simplicity, "She am evrywhir, lad."

and with a belly shaped like a failed dumpling hanging precariously over a string belt. He was also very heavily armed with an array of sharp objects.

Beyond the Doorway

"'Alt," he commanded. "'Oo the 'ell goos thir?"

"Earthworm sits in ash tree," replied Dandy cheerfully. The creature immediately saluted and stepped back to let us pass, though not without shooting us a warning glare. "That am our GOTE," said Dandy over his shoulder, as if this were an explanation. "Sweet lad when yo get to know 'im."

"He doesn't look much like any go—"

"Guardian of the Outer Tunnel Elf. We'm big on acronyms, being small. Us, now, us is the NUDE(S) rep."[2] I didn't like to ask but just had a horrifyingly embarrassing vision of what might be expected of us later, Mother Earth being so, well, natural. Presently, we came to a junction with several tunnels fanning off in different directions and Dandy pointed us towards one.

---

[2] National Union of Devas and Elves (Smestow branch). Obviously.

"Yo goo in thir forra bit while us checks as she'll see yo. It's tay break so yo can 'ave a sit down. Mrs T will see yo all right."

Whistling merrily, he disappeared and left us to enter a cavernous chamber dotted with rough stone tables and chairs at which sat a motley crew of elves munching carrot cake and regarding us with a mixture of curiosity and hostility. Humans were evidently not among their favourite beings. Mrs T poured out two tiny cups of some dark and aromatic herbal brew and pushed them across to us without a word. It was revolting but we smiled graciously anyway and gazed around the room nervously. For the most part, the assorted elves were dressed in baggy, mud-stained working clothes and woolly hats; long, curved noses, big ears and dimples abounded, as did some very strange accents that began to growl louder until, to our great relief, a high-pitched whistle sounded and the company shuffled out back to work, giving us a wide berth.

"I don't think I like it here," whispered Gaynor. "Can you get me out of this?" She was sitting with legs tightly crossed and arms clasped about herself, a pleading expression all over her face. I assumed an authoritative frown, of the sort people have when they want to appear deeply thoughtful and totally in control, as I wondered how grateful she would be. But my machinations were cut short by Dandy's sudden reappearance. He was now wearing a smart, if slightly creased, royal blue tunic embellished with shiny buttons and rather too much gold braid, and shiny black gumboots. His tufty hair was neatly parted and an attempt had been made to slick it down at the sides.

"Right, ower kids, am yo ready? Us 'as fixed it up. Do yo' think yo' could tidy yo'sen up a bit? Yo's that riffy. It ent done to visit 'Erself lookin' like a lummock."

We smartened ourselves up and brushed ourselves down, I tucked my shirt in and Gaynor tossed her hair out, and we warily followed Dandy along another long, brightly lit passage being challenged frequently by GITs.

"Hedgehog dives in pond."

"Butterfly takes biscuit."

"Rabbit sits on barn owl."

Finally we arrived at the outer chamber of the inner sanctum where an appropriately musty earthiness hung in the air and rainwater rich in sulphated nitrites dripped down the walls. We held our breath as an imposing wooden door was flung open with an exaggerated flourish by a warty elf in tight green breeches and purple smock.

"Her Royal Highness, Most Excellent and Gracious Majesty, Creator of All Natural Beauty, Ruler of the Underground, Middleground, Seas and What's-Left-Of the Overground, to Whom be All Honour and Allegiance of Small Peoples Everywhere... Mother!"

Gaynor gripped my hand painfully and we both froze, then gulped a bit and looked helplessly at each other.

"Goo on then," urged Dandy. "Stop yer slummockin'. Yo'll 'ave it dark." He gave us both a discreet but effective kick on the ankles. We went in and stood foolishly gazing around until a vague wave from the far corner caught my eye.

"Do approach," said a rich and loamy voice that echoed round the sanctum and set the candelabras rattling. We set off in that direction until at last we saw her, Mother Earth, a tiny point-like almost spherical figure swathed in green velvet robes, perched on the dark blue cushions of a huge throne that reached from floor to ceiling. Tiny legs hung loosely over the brocade and the wave of her thin hand was almost the only sign of life about her.

"Come on, come on," she spoke again, taking us aback with the fruity strength of her voice. Well, we were a little at a loss to know how to behave, it not being every day that one meets a Creator of All Natural Beauty when we were only just getting used to the idea of Dandy. I tried a sort of bow.

"We are honoured to be received by Your Royal Highness." I find there's nothing like a bit of servility to endear one to strangers.

"Yes, you are," she boomed back with a faint nod of what we could now see were several chins. "And don't bother with the Royal Highness bit. Most Excellent and Gracious Majesty will do fine. Well now," she waved us to a couple of nearby stone seats, "it's always nice to get visitors, even human ones. I just hope you're not going to write any silly poems when you go back outside. I mean, daffodils are all very well but they're hardly the point, are they?"

"No poems, I promise, Most Excell—"

"Yes, this sort of visit is all too infrequent these days. Time was, everyone wanted to talk to Us and We could even wander about Upstairs without being taken for a rabbit and shot at but hardly any of you seem to know We exist now, which is most unflattering since after all, don't forget, We were here first and if it wasn't for Us and Our people there wouldn't be any mountains and rivers and fields and trees and animals and, might We add with all humility, people." She paused for breath. I didn't suppose she was about to let us in on the exact details of human evolution despite this bait (and even if she had, you could hardly expect me to announce how I came by the knowledge).

"Indeed, Most Ex—"

"No, it's all changed now. You people never give Us a thought, too busy ripping up the kingdom, pouring concrete down holes, rushing about in those noisy car-things and putting up those house-things like mushrooms. I mean, there'll be no green places left soon. Couldn't you get them to stop it, eh, eh?" She was quivering with emotion, the chins rolling ominously.

"I don't think we can do much ourselves, Most—"

"And we have to have somewhere to live and places to work," added Gaynor, warming to the debate.

"Yes, yes, We know that, lassie, We know that." Mother's voice went up a couple of octaves, making us shrink back on our stones. "But must you ruin My world doing it? You used to be perfectly happy in caves, didn't you, and they fitted in perfectly well with everything else."

"Cold, draughty, uncomfortable and not enough to go round," Gaynor countered with conviction, as though she had personal experience.

"Ah well, lassie, that's the root of it. There's just too many of you."

"It's the spirit of nature," I observed sadly, my mind flashing back to the moment before Dandy's appearance.

"No need for smut, young man."

"And anyway, we do use natural materials for our houses and machines and stuff." Gaynor clearly had the obstinate spirit of a farm-er's daughter and wasn't going to let herself be browbeaten, even by a Most Excellent and Gracious Majesty. I looked across at her with new respect. "There's sand and cement," she went on, "and iron and copper and… um, gold." She glanced down wistfully at her left hand as Mother leaned forward and peered closely at her.

"We'll grant you that, girl. You're obviously the intelligent one here. We only usually get mystics visiting Us and We never have the faintest idea what they're going on about. Give Us a headache, they do." She paused to fan herself with a willow leaf before warming to her message. "Anyway, since we're onto fundamentals, do try to see Our point of view. The fact is that your people and Mine find themselves tacitly at war. No—" she held up a tiny hand as we both opened our mouths to object "—it's true. You're trampling over everything We've done and upsetting the balance of it all. When the devas can't grow anything they get very disgruntled and We don't mind saying it's getting serious now – much more of it and We won't be able to hold them back. The Earth must save Herself. There'll be drought and flood and eruptions and disease…"

I'm sure I could see the tiniest of tears form at the corner of one eye. There was a long silence as Gaynor and I slumped, suitably chastened and bearing the brunt of this on behalf of our entire species. Finally, Mother heaved herself to a wobbly upright position and dropped down to the ground, beckoning us to follow her to an anteroom behind the throne. We followed silently at a distance, being very careful not to tread on her.

"No time for idle chatter." She waved a hand towards the two armed elves at a heavy oak door and they stepped back saluting smartly as it creaked open on huge iron hinges. "We'll just show you the Archive Office. You'll soon get the picture. But," she definitely winked, "take care, We have a rather special, er, filing system."

It was indeed special. We entered the room and another era, finding ourselves standing high in snow-capped mountains overlooking a young, dark Earth beneath racing thick clouds. Then the skies were ripped open by electric arcs that thundered to the ground, green shoots springing out where they touched whilst trees ripped up through the earth, mushroomed green and were stripped bare in a moment, every scene passing in the blink of an eye. There was inconceivable colour, fiery red dawns and golden sunsets giving way to the blackest nights decorated by billions of bright stars. And as light returned, all across the wide veldt below an unimaginable number of animal species roamed, grazing the plants and trees or drinking at clear blue lakesides as huge birds flew in all directions. Distant mountains grew, heaved and were carved apart by torrential rivers of water and ice, great vaults opened up in the ground and then healed over, the sun burned and the air shimmered and the plains became a desert where scorpions scurried before rains swept through and gave birth to new forests. Fertility coursed across the land, twisting and weaving in a plexus of new-born plants and flowers, animals and fish.

"Oh no, look," Gaynor whispered in my ear, gripping my arm.

A group of men appeared hesitantly from the trees, eating from the branches and the plants below, until there were many of them forming into groups, sheltering in the hills as they made clothes and tools. They protected one another, bowed to the sun and made friends with small nature creatures who showed them how to find the fertility paths, where the people danced and built stone monuments and storehouses. And as they became powerful and many, the groups split and fought each other for control of the stores. The animals of the plain were caged and then eaten. Stone temples fell into ruin as cities grew and the men realised that they could master the world and become wealthy and comfortable and overcome their weaknesses by using everything in the earth to build machines and power stations, filling the air with acrid smoke and the rivers with waste.

The snake of fertility began to drag itself weakly, the Earth grew empty patches and the seas became acidic as the men tried desperately to postpone their death by fighting one another for food, for land, for control as despairing nature creatures raced here and there to patch the world back together. A thunderous storm gathered overhead and lightning flashed aimlessly, with rivers flooding, volcanos spewing fire and cracks opening in the seabed sending mountainous waves to wipe away shorelines. Gaynor and I recoiled towards the door with the stench of disease filling our nostrils as the scene before us shrivelled into utter chaos. And above the noise I heard a rich, earthy voice scream.

"Rape!"

We must have passed out because, when I opened my eyes, Gaynor and I were wrapped in each other's arms lying in a grassy hollow beside the Smestow. She smiled at me and opened her lips to speak, then hurriedly pushed me away and sat up straight, pulling her dress down as close to her knees as it would go before gulping a bit and pointing over my shoulder. Dandy sat on the edge of the hollow observing us thoughtfully.

"I... er, I thought it was a dream," she whispered hoarsely.

"Nahhh, bab, 's all real." His voice was quiet and his face drooped in sadness. "See, yo was right to think on 'bout what yo want. Wishin' for things am all well an' good but in the end—" he paused to slide down the grass and then haul himself up onto my knee "—it am all a matter of love." He fixed me with a meaningful stare. "Things am bad, right enough. But what keeps everything gooin' – yo an' me an' every other daft aypeth – is Mother's love."

Gaynor nodded, deep in thought, and then seemed to come to a decision, jumping to her feet and standing above us on the brow of the hollow, causing Dandy to shield his eyes and my blood pressure to soar dangerously.

"You're right, Dandy. All this—" she swept her arms wide "—is awful and we must do something about it. Enough. We'll start here and now. I wish that this filthy, stinking canal could be clear and clean again with fish swimming in it and wild flowers growing all along the bank. There!"

Dandy slid down my leg and puffed himself up, eyes alight and arms outstretched, poised to fulfil his promise. But I was horrified and also scrambled to my feet.

"Wait a minute," I protested, "don't waste it all by being hasty. Look, I mean, I do wish you hadn't said that." Dandy froze in mid-performance then let his arms and mouth droop again dejectedly.

"An' us," he sighed, his voice a gentle breeze as he faded from view, "wish as 'ow us 'ad never started this. Tara a bit."

All of which accounts, I believe, for why the Smestow branch of the Staffs and Worcs is still in a class of its own, a long and limp, sickly pea-green stretch of water that leaves me totally unimpressed. And why my lost love Gaynor has never spoken to me again since that day.

196

If you have enjoyed this book...

Local Legend is committed to publishing the very best spiritual writing, both fiction and non-fiction. You might also enjoy:

BROKEN SEA
Nigel Peace (ISBN 978-1-910027-23-3)

In the summer of 1968, at the height of joyful revolution in the West, darker reactionary clouds are gathering elsewhere... Preparing for university, Roy falls helplessly in love for the first time. This is a good thing. Unfortunately, Eva is Czech and her homeland is about to be savagely invaded by the military forces of the Warsaw Pact. This is now a struggle for identity, both personal and national, where neither love nor freedom are tolerated. In the course of one heady and dramatic year, everyone will be profoundly changed.

5* "Packed full of political tension... excellent characterisation and a gripping plot. Highly recommended." The Wishing Shelf Book Awards

SIGNS OF LIFE
Nigel Peace (ISBN 978-1-907203-20-6)

What's it all about, then? Life. Is there any point and does anybody have a plan? Well, actually they do but it's not very well thought out and it seems that Heaven is uncomfortably like Earth, with the same idiotic people and ridiculous bureaucracy. The angels mean well but their Grand Plan for humanity is just begging to be sabotaged...

Join our heroes on a breathtaking journey between worlds involving lost identities, car chases, roulette, the delivery of fish and some SEx (but not as you know it). And a nice dog.

TWO SISTERS
Graham Adrian (ISBN 978-1-910027-32-5)

Graham's debut novel, based on a Suffolk legend, is a brilliant, historically accurate description of Georgian times including genuine dialect. But far more than this, it is a truly exciting and uniquely spiritual adventure story. Nance is an honest and hard-working farmer's daughter, but falling in love only begins a sequence of devastating events that seem to lead inevitably to the gallows! Yet she is watched over by her sister's loving spirit in the afterlife, doing all she can to avert the consequences of Nance's reckless decisions. Every character in this gripping story, illustrated with period images, leaps from the pages as we recognise ourselves in them.

A SINGLE PETAL
Oliver Eade (ISBN 978-1-907203-42-8)

Winner of the national Local Legend *Spiritual Writing Competition*, this page-turner is a story of murder, politics and passion set in ancient China. Yet its themes of loyalty, commitment and deep personal love are every bit as relevant for us today as they were in past times. The author is an expert on Chinese culture and history, and his debut adult novel deserves to become a classic.

"An intriguing mystery… Highly recommended."
The Wishing Shelf Book Awards.

A MESSAGE FROM SOURCE
Grace Gabriella Puskas (ISBN 978-1-910027-00-4)

Beautiful and inspiring poetry of the Spirit that reaches deep within the consciousness, awakening the reader to higher states of awareness, spiritual connection and love. The author, in familiar and thoughtful language, explores the power of meditation, the nature of the universe and of time, our place within the environment and who we truly are as creative beings of light and sound.

Winner of the Local Legend national *Spiritual Writing Competition*.

PATHWAYS OF THE DRUIDS
Christopher J Pine (ISBN 978-1-907203-61-9)

Christopher's wonderful debut novel is an exciting blend of fantasy, myth and true history – a page-turning adventure story for all ages. The Roman Empire occupies Britannia and the ancient culture and freedoms of the Celts are being destroyed. Yet the Druid priests have a mastery of nature and magical skills. They devise a final, desperate strategy to avoid slavery by opening a portal into an alternative world, and the last Celtic tribe races to cross the threshold before it is too late…

THE HOUSE OF BEING
Peter Walker (ISBN 978-1-910027-26-4)

Acutely observed verse by a master of his craft, showing us the mind, the body and the soul of what it is to be human in this glorious natural world. A linguist and a priest, the author takes us deep beneath the surface of life and writes with sensitivity, compassion and, often, with searing wit and self-deprecation. This is a collection the reader will return to again and again.

A winner of our national *Spiritual Writing Competition*.

DAY TRIPS TO HEAVEN
T J Hobbs (ISBN 978-1-907203-99-2)

The author's debut novel is a brilliant description of life in the spiritual worlds and of the guidance available to all of us on Earth as we struggle to be the best we can. Ethan is learning to be a spirit guide but having a hard time of it, with too many questions and too much self-doubt. But he has potential, so is given a special dispensation to bring a few deserving souls for a preview of the afterlife, to help them with crucial decisions they have to make in their lives. The book is full of gentle humour, compassion and spiritual knowledge, and it asks important questions of us all.

CELESTIAL AMBULANCE
Ann Matkins (ISBN 978-1-907203-45-9)

A brave and delightful comedy novel. Having died of cancer, Ben wakes up in the afterlife looking forward to a good rest, only to find that everyone is expected to get a job! He becomes the driver of an ambulance (with a mind of her own), rescuing the spirits of others who have died suddenly and delivering them safely home. This book is as thought-provoking as it is entertaining.

"A fun novel packed full of wisdom."
The Wishing Shelf Book Awards.

INDIGO AWAKES
Stephanie de Winter (ISBN 978-1-907203-44-2)

Indigo's life is going nowhere. She is tired and depressed, abused by both her partner and her employer. But then a strong, quiet voice within demands change and soon intense dreams and everyday synchronicities show her an alternative path. With courage and determination, she battles her demons and embarks on a journey of spiritual awakening that transforms her life. Stephanie's stunning debut novel vibrates with energy, as beautifully written as it is inspiring. And its sequel, *Indigo Haunted* (ISBN 978-1-907203-78-7) takes Indigo's story even further to a genuinely exciting and dramatic finale.

REDEEMING LUCIFER
Lennart Svensson (ISBN 978-1-910027-20-2)

This extraordinary novel, the author's debut in English, is a gripping spiritual adventure in the finest tradition of legendary deeds, blending esotericism, pure imagination and acutely-observed historical fact. Our heroes journey through parallel, mystical worlds on an epic quest to find Lucifer, no less, and to heal the world of its ills. But first, they must fight the ultimate cosmic battle... This book challenges each of us to examine the deeper purposes of our lives.

Local Legend titles are available as paperbacks and eBooks.
Further details and extracts of these and many
other beautiful books for the Mind, Body and Spirit
may be seen at
www.local-legend.co.uk

www.ingramcontent.com/pod-product-compliance
Lightning Source LLC
Chambersburg PA
CBHW060436180626
46817CB00007B/2839

9 781910 027455